LOOT!

Also by Albert Payson Terhune
in Large Print:

Grudge Mountain
The Critter
Lad: A Dog
Lad of Sunnybank
The Way of a Dog

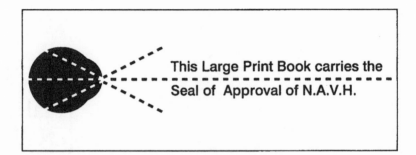

LOOT!

Albert Payson Terhune

G.K. Hall & Co. • **Thorndike, Maine**

Published in 2000 by arrangement with HarperCollins Publishers,
Inc.

This story originally appeared serially
under the title of *THE LOOTERS*.

G.K. Hall Large Print Perennial Bestsellers Series.

The text of this Large Print edition is unabridged.
Other aspects of the book may vary from the original edition.

Set in 16 pt. Plantin.

Printed in the United States on permanent paper.

Library of Congress Cataloging-in-Publication Data

Terhune, Albert Payson, 1872–1942.
    Loot! / by Albert Payson Terhune.
       p.   cm.
    ISBN 0-7838-8746-9 (lg. print : hc : alk. paper)
    1. Collie — Fiction.   2. Dogs — Fiction.   3. Large type books.
I. Title.
PS3539.E65 L66 2000
813'.52—dc21   00-020840

LOOT!

Chapter I

As Brant Hildreth topped the steep rise of the hill-pasture ridge, the meadow and its crazily twisting little brook lay directly beneath him. The sight of the winding snarl of water gave the man a thrill known only to born trout fishermen when, on the opening day of the season, they sight a brook which gives high promise of sport.

It was Hildreth's first half holiday since he had come back to his home county of Preakness in the North Jersey hinterland, nearly two months earlier. During that time he had been slaving, night and day. He felt he had earned the right to an hour or two with rod and fly, in the streamlet where, in his boyhood, trout had been plentiful and pugnacious.

At his heels trotted his corn-colored young collie, Thane; gaily eager for whatever fun this tramp with his master might bring forth.

(A collie is by no means an ideal companion on a trout-fishing expedition, having merry tendencies toward chasing a fly-cast and splashing noisily into the pools. Thence every trout is scared by his advent.)

Thane was a privileged character, so far as Brant Hildreth was concerned. So, when the

7

collie had dashed out of the office through a carelessly opened door and had caught the man's trail and danced delightedly up to him, Brant had not had the heart to order him home.

A smear of red against the soft green of the springtime meadow caught Hildreth's eye, as he paused at the ridgetop to survey the snake-like coil of brook below him. His forehead puckered into a frown. Early as he was, another fisherman was ahead of him. That meant a dividing of the territory, at best. At worst, it meant that the firstcomer might have been clumsy enough to scare a half-mile's trout population to the bottom of the deepest pools and render them blind to the lure of the most tempting fly.

Then he saw that the fisher was a woman, clad in waders and short tweed skirt and sweater, her head surmounted by a flaring scarlet tam-o'-shanter. This bright hat was the patch of red which had drawn his notice. Right deftly she was casting, the brook water swirling around her booted knees.

But Brant gave scant heed to her skill. At a half-turn of her daintily poised head, he saw her profile, and he recognized her. He had taken a stride forward. Now he slid to a worried halt.

"Thane," he muttered, half-aloud, as the collie came running back, inquiringly, to see why his master did not continue his descent of the steep slope, "Thane, I left this gorgeous country, seven years ago, on account of *her*. And, ever since I've been back here, I've been bracing myself to meet her. They told me she was away somewhere on a visit, Thane. But there she is. Well — it had to come, soon or late!"

He let his voice trail away. Like many another lonely man he had gotten into the habit of talking to this big young dog of his, at times, as to a fellow human; even though he realized that the collie could not understand one word in ten that his master spoke. Hildreth fell silent, broodingly staring down at the red-hatted girl. The dog beside him fidgeted to be on the go again.

The lush meadow and the fire-blue brook and the encircling Ramapo Mountains and the nearer orchards with their snow-and-pink burden of blossoms, faded from Brant's unnoting eyes; displaced by a confused jumble of more vivid mental pictures — pictures which had an exasperating way of centering around this girl at the waterside below him.

Preakness is a rural county. Its seat and biggest town is Sark, a rambling settlement with a population of something under five thousand. Several families there date back to colonial days; among them the Hildreths and the Cormicks, both old-time patroons and folk of vast local import.

For two centuries the Cormicks and the Hildreths had been close friends. Brant's own father had begun life as the law partner of Emmons Cormick, richest man in Preakness County. But with that generation the ancient friendship died. Emmons Cormick's only son, Ralph, was some years older than Brant. From boyhood, the two had not gotten on well together.

Their lack of affection for each other was not improved when Brant, at twenty, fell headlong in love with sixteen-year-old Kay Cormick, Ralph's sister. Ralph spent much time and shrewdness in making the callow suitor ridiculous in the girl's eyes. At last, he had become so offensive in his attitude toward Hildreth as to provoke an open breach between the two families.

Kay had sided with her brother. With a fine sense of eternal heartbreak, Brant had shaken the dust of Sark from his shoes and had gone to New York to seek his fortune. He did not find fortune, in any large quantities. He found a job as a reporter on the New York *Chronicle* and he remained in newspaper work for the next seven years.

Then, loath to leave his widowed mother alone in the rambling old Hildreth house and acquiring a few thousand dollars by the sale of a strip of land to the railroad, Brant had come back to Sark and had bought the local weekly newspaper, the *Bugle*. His loved father was gone. Bit by bit, all the Hildreth fortune was gone, too, except an annuity which kept his mother in semi-comfort.

Emmons Cormick was dead, too. His son, Ralph, ruled as head of the depleted Cormick clan; dwelling with his sister, Kay. They reigned in the colonial homestead, from which Brant had stamped in loverly misery, seven years ago, vowing never again to set foot in the abode where he had been shamed and affronted.

He could look back over that hysterical boyish rage now, with a smile. But the smile held more than a trace of bitterness. Not bitterness toward the girl who had been little more than a child, but against the bullying elder brother who had taken such pains to make him absurd and to set Kay against him.

This had been one of the strongest if most secret motives for Brant's purchase of the half-defunct *Bugle*. His own father, as county judge, had done manful work in making Preakness County clean and graftless and in building up its natural resources and in stimulating it to healthy growth. Since his death, the county's affairs had drifted into the hands of local politicians. Openly they were exploiting it for their own gain. One of these local magnates was young Ralph Cormick, chairman of the Board of Freeholders and —nominally at least — a political leader of the county.

The *Bugle*, a half-century earlier, had been a mighty influence for good. Brant believed the dying newspaper could be made so again; that it could be swung as a club over the gang which misruled Preakness County, to beat them into decency and to eliminate their thriving graft and incompetence and to replace corruption by sane and thrifty government.

Yet the knowledge that Ralph Cormick was in the forefront of the looters added tenfold to the grim zest wherewith Brant was undertaking his mighty task. It would be a keen joy to square himself with his olden foe, by honest methods, and, at the same time to cleanse the county of its ever-increasing blots.

As he stood musing, Brant was aware of an unwonted bit of motion, at some distance beyond the brook, a constant fretful movement which the corner of his eye registered for some time without communicating itself to his brain. Now he came out of his reverie and focused his gaze on it.

The meadow was cut in two, at some distance beyond the brook, by a high old-fashioned rail fence. On the far side a dozen cattle were browsing eagerly on the fresh young grass, after the long winter's fare of hay and silo. One of these cattle, a Holstein bull, had strayed to the boundary fence. There, with industrious horns and butting head and rubbing shoulders, he was trying to open a gap in the rickety rails.

It was this incessant motion which had attracted Hildreth's notice.

The bull intermitted his fence-smashing maneuvers by stepping back occasionally and, with head lowered, pawing the earth with one and another of his restless forefeet.

Brant gave only scant heed to the big brute's antics. Apparently the giant black-and-white Holstein was in a bad temper, and he was venting his ill-humor by lunging at the fence and by worrying its rails with his thick horns.

"Thane," said Hildreth, "we worked till almost daylight, down at that scrubby office, so we could have this morning for fishing. And now, let's turn around and go back to work again. Probably, I'm due to meet her, some-where, sometime, somehow, on the street. But I'm not going to do it purposely. That's why you and I are going to sneak back, the way we came, before she happens to look up and see us, Thane, old friend. Rotten bad luck, isn't it? — Not that I care, one way or the other, about her, Thane. I put her out of my memory, ever so long ago. Still, it isn't pleasant to meet anyone you've been made ridiculous to; anyone who has condemned you on other people's say-so, Thane. So let's beat it."

Usually, when Hildreth talked to him, the corn-colored collie would stand looking up in wistful curiosity at his master, plumed tail awag, head on one side and tulip ears cocked, waiting for the frequent repetition of his own name, which always delighted him.

But, now, he gave no heed at all to the man's half-mumbled words; even though the word "Thane," was repeated so often. Instead, the

13

dog was gazing fixedly down the hillslope. His wiry body was rigid. Something was absorbing every atom of his attention, even to the exclusion of Brant's loved voice.

"If you're hoping I'll take you down there to be patted and made much of by her, Thane," reproved Hildreth, "you've got another guess coming. She has a dog of her own — or rather her sweet brother, Ralph, has. A great police dog that he calls 'Mowgli.' She doesn't need to add you to her list of hangers-on. So, come along. We've —"

Thane interrupted the man's reproof — to which the collie had paid no notice — by a resonant growl, far down in his throat. His hackles were abristle now. His body was tensed and crouching. More closely, Brant followed the direction of the deepset dark eyes in their stern gaze. He saw Thane was not looking at Kay Cormick at all, but at the Holstein bull on the far side of the fence.

As Brant glanced again at the bull, he saw the black-and-white monster draw back a step or two and launch himself at the panel of half-rotten fence which he had been assailing. Under the weight and impetus of his rush, the panel crumpled like wet cardboard.

Through the gap plunged the bull.

Then it was that Hildreth realized what had roused the grazing brute's temper from chronic sullenness to acute murder. Under the bright morning sun, Kay Cormick's flaming scarlet tam-o'-shanter had caught his eyes. Even as the *capeador*'s red cloak rouses the fury of bulls in the Spanish *corridas,* so did the vivid hat awaken the Holstein to crazy rage.

Wherefore, he had worked away at the weakest panel of the high rail fence until he had undermined it for his rush. Then he had hammered down the only barrier between him and his prey.

With queer canine intuition, Thane had guessed the bull's fiery purpose.

Kay Cormick, her back to the fence, continued to cast deftly into the pool at whose verge she stood. The wind was the other way and blew back from her the muffled crash of the falling fence panel and the thud of sharp hoofs on the soft earth. The swirl and slap of water around her knees and the chuckle and purl of the brook deadened these more distant warnings.

Hildreth cast aside his rod and creel and fly book; and sprinted down the hill. But, at his first step he knew he could not reach the galloping bull before the Holstein should have covered the hundred yards between the fence and the unseeing girl. Even could he do so, he would be powerless — unarmed as he was — to avert from Kay that ton of onrushing piebald death.

As he ran, his heart sick with hideous apprehension, he was aware, as in a blinding flash, that he had lied to himself when he said he had

15

put this slenderly graceful girl out of his heart and out of his memory. Once and for all he knew, past every future doubt, that all his life was bound up in hers. Yes, and with the revelation came the knowledge that she was about to be trampled and gored into mangled lifelessness; while he, who would have laid down a dozen lives for her, was helpless to come to her aid.

Then, ahead of him on the slope he saw something tearing along, stomach to earth — something which whizzed onward like a streak of yellow flame.

Thane had not waited for orders. The spirits of ten thousand cattle-herding ancestors called to him from the misty recesses of his queer collie brain, telling him what to do and how to do it. As the fence tumbled down, Thane had gone into action, lightning swift, unerring, unafraid.

Chapter II

Hildreth saw the dog reach the bottom of the slope and the margin of the brook. He saw Thane clear the brook at its widest in one flying leap, and, without breaking his stride, dash full at the fast-galloping bull.

At the same moment, Kay Cormick heard the muted thunder of hoofs on the soft turf behind her. She turned to find the Holstein bearing down upon her, less than forty feet away. No scope for flight nor even for dodging from the path of that bovine cyclone! White as ashes, the girl stood waiting her fate.

Then, past her, whizzed the streak of sunlit gold, as Thane flew straight at the charging monster's lowered black head.

It was a gallant spectacle — the sixty-pound collie rushing to meet the onslaught of a creature nearly forty times his weight and many times his size — a creature whose horns and hoofs were terrible weapons of offense as opposed to the single set of jaws which are a dog's only armament.

Not in tragic martyrdom did Thane oppose his puny bulk to the irresistible brute. True, he had growled worriedly at the menace, when the

17

Holstein had been weakening the barrier fence. But, as soon as the call for action, he had flung himself into the fearsomely unequal battle with a gay zest, as though he were in a jolly romp with his master.

He was no fool, this impetuously galloping collie. He was not minded to lose his chance of rescuing the girl and to sacrifice his own glad life by clashing, head on, with his tremendous adversary. He was opposing brain to brawn. The prospect delighted him.

When he was within three feet of the onthundering bull, Thane shifted ever so slightly in his stride. The huge lowered head missed him, clean. The nearest horn barely ruffled his corn-colored coat. Then, still at full momentum, Thane gripped the bull's ear, and held on. His own impetus swung him clean around, so that his furry body slapped against the Holstein's shoulder. But he did not release that ear-grip.

As a result, the bull felt a sharp anguish in his ear. At the same time, he felt himself jerked sharply sidewise by the impact of a flying sixty-pound weight. The jar and the pain threw him ever so little to the right. On he thundered, past Kay Cormick. The raking horns missed her by a matter of inches. The butting left shoulder knocked her off balance as it brushed past her.

A bull charges always with eyes tight shut — a fact to which many a matador owes his own continued existence. Missing Kay and floundering into the pool, the Holstein turned, opening his eyes.

As he did so, the weight and the grinding pain were gone from his ear, to be replaced within a fraction of a second by a tenfold more anguishing grip that shore its way deep into his sensitive nostrils.

Thane had changed holds, even while the bull was turning to renew the attack on Kay. Now, for an instant, he hung to the pain-tossed nose of the Holstein, before dropping lightly to earth and diving between the stamping fore-legs.

He slashed the vast underbody cruelly with one of his curved white eyeteeth, as he darted out again. Then, another nip at the bleeding nostrils, and he had sunk his teeth into the bull's other ear, as his enemy launched himself afresh at the wearer of the maddening red hat.

Again, weight and leverage and pain and a sharp sidewise wrench spoiled the accuracy of the charge. Again the tortured nostrils were rent.

The bull halted, momentarily, to reconstruct his plan of campaign. As avid as ever to stamp upon and gore the fiery hat's wearer, yet he re-alized dimly that something golden and tor-mentingly punitive kept flashing between him and his victim.

Before he could hope to slaughter the scarlet-crowned human with any comfort, it seemed he must get rid of this harrowing dog. It would be

19

an easy matter to brush so puny an opponent from his way, if once he should concentrate on the task. So the Holstein wheeled and charged the collie. With head down and with reechoing bellows he hurled himself at the gaily waiting Thane.

At the same instant, Kay felt her pretty new tam-o'-shanter snatched rudely from her head. She was swung about. A man's stocky body interposed itself between her and the bull.

Brant Hildreth had run to her, at the top of his trained athletic speed, down the precipitous ridge slope. He had reached the scene of strife several seconds too late to have been of service to the girl, had not Thane intervened to save her. But he was on hand now, to do what he might, should the bull burst past Thane's ever-shifting agile guard. His first motion was to seize the offending hat; his next to thrust Kay behind him.

"Quick!" he ordered. "Run for the fence. It's your tam, not you, he's after. Quick!"

Brandishing the provocative scarlet headgear, Brant stepped toward the Holstein, waving it. He felt he could trust to his own swiftness of foot and his dodging prowess to keep out of the bull's way until the girl should reach the safety of the fence and thus the highway beyond. He believed he could do it, if she would move fast enough.

But, as he turned to look back at her, over his shoulder, he saw Kay had not stirred. Still

20

dazed by the sudden peril, she was eying him in blank astonishment. The bull, however, did not share her physical apathy. The insulting waving of the flary red tam set him into fresh and ferocious motion. He charged the man who flourished the hat so teasingly at him.

But, this time, the Holstein did not so much as get into his stride, before the collie was all over him. Now that his adored master, and not a stranger, was in peril, Thane flew to the assault with maniac zeal. He tore the ragged nostrils, he rent the bleeding ears, he slashed for the eyes; he was everywhere in general and nowhere in particular. He was a flaming instrument of torture for the harassed bull.

Again, the Holstein seemed to realize he must annihilate the dog before he could wreak his murder lust on a human. He whirled about and sought to crush Thane into the earth with his huge forehead. But, when the curled and shaggy front smote the ground, Thane was not there. The dog sprang lightly over the descending head and landed on the bull's heaving shoulders.

Thence, after driving his jaws hastily but conscientiously into the flesh above the spine, he leaped down again. By the time he had touched ground, he had nipped the nearest heel, viciously. Then his teeth met in the swishing tail.

It was pretty work, and it did sharp damage. The bull roared with the agony of it and butted confusedly at the prancing dog, only to get another slash in the nostrils. Back sprang Thane from the Holstein's lumbering onset. The collie's hindfeet slipped on the blood-greasy turf. He fell sprawling.

Immediately, the bull was at him. But a collie down is not a collie beaten. Thane tucked his legs under him and rolled nimbly to one side, barely avoiding the rake of the deadly horns and the flailing forehoofs. As he sprang upward, he slashed deeply the underbody that plunged above him, sprang free of it and nipped the hock which all but brained him.

Then again he was all over his foe.

It dawned on the bull that this form of conflict had lasted quite long enough. He was fat. The winter's stall confinement had left him short of breath. He had been through an uncomfortable amount of lively motion, during the past few moments; and he was undergoing a horrible quantity of unrepaid torture. Nor was he able to get within butting or stamping distance of his eel-like antagonist.

His first red anger was giving place to a bewildered fear. He ceased his series of abortive charges and lunges, and moved a pace backward. As though his withdrawal were a signal for a fresh impetus, Thane attacked him with gay destructiveness, seeking out the several most hurtable parts of the Holstein's tough anatomy, and scoring them again and again.

Confusion gave place to fright, in the bull's heart. He swung about and fled. On every side of him and behind him raged Thane. With seeming aimlessness the collie drove him. Yet, in a few seconds, the bull found himself cantering with loud bellows through the gap where he had broken down the fence panel.

Thane did not carry the pursuit farther. Panting, wagging his tail, grinning in high glee, he stood in the gap, looking at Brant for commendation of his merry exploit.

Before going back to where Kay stood, Hildreth crossed to the fence. First stooping to catch Thane's classic head roughly between his own hands and speak a half-dozen breathless words of praise, he lifted up the fence panel, as best he could, and put it into place. Though he knew there was little fear of the Holstein's renewing the attack, yet he did not care to chance another scene like the one he had just gone through.

Then, realizing he still held Kay Cormick's tam bunched tightly in his fist, he went sulkily toward the brook. But already she had come more than half the way to meet him. Her bronzed little face was pallid and her hands were not wholly steady. Yet she forced herself to smile as she greeted the man.

"Brant!" she exclaimed.

Then, puzzled by his glum demeanor, she went on:

"Brant Hildreth! Don't you remember me? I'm —"

"Of course I do," he made sullen reply;

23

adding: "I'm sorry I had to snatch your hat off like that. But it was the hat he was after. I — I hope I haven't spoiled it."

The smile left her dark eyes, as she spoke, shudderingly:

"And you not only snatched it away, Brant; but you ran up to him, waving it in his very face. That was playing with death. It —"

"Death had just been playing with *you*," he returned, monstrous ill at ease under her look. "So I took a turn at it, to give you a breathing space. At that, if you have any thanks to throw away, they aren't mine. You can thank Thane, here. He seems to be the only hero of the day. I wasn't in any danger, you know. Neither were you, after Thane began his work. He —"

He paused. The girl had dropped to her knees. She threw both arms around the collie's neck, hugging him.

"You wonderful gorgeous hero dog!" she cried, brokenly. "If it hadn't been for you —"

Getting hold of her frayed nerves, she rose to her feet again as Thane backed annoyedly away from the strangling and undesired hug. He was not fond of indiscriminate affection — few collies are — nor did he choose to be mauled by strangers. His commonsensible reception of her advances served like a dash of ice water, to bring Kay back to normal.

"I'm afraid your fishing is pretty well ruined for the morning," continued Brant. "So is mine, for that matter. My rod and creel and my

24

book of flies are up yonder, somewhere. I didn't even notice I dropped them. It serves me right, for running away to fish, when I ought to be at my desk. Denny will probably get the paper into a nice libel suit or two, while I'm gone. He yearns to be a great editor, and his chief idea of writing seems to be vituperation. He scribbles, every minute my back is turned. Today, probably, he —"

"Denny?" she queried. "Is he a Sark man? I don't know anyone named Denny, here. But then so many new people —"

"He's new," assented Hildreth. "Brand new. The very newest. And Denny isn't 'people,' either. He's just 'folks.' His full name is Dennis Blayne. He used to be a pork-and-beans prize fighter — a good one, too, I've, heard — at the same time he was a composing-room roustabout on the *Chronicle*, where I was a reporter. By and by he graduated to the linotype machines. And he turned out to be one of the best operators the paper had. A second Johnny Ruton. He's a typical East-side tough, outwardly; but he is all sorts of a good scout, when you know him."

Chapter III

Brant was glad to keep the talk on such neutral grounds, until he could find excuse to get away from the presence of this girl who awoke such bittersweet memories and who so utterly had overthrown all his years of resolution to forget her.

"Yes," he meandered on, sparring for time, "Denny is a character. I ran across him again, when I was in New York trying to get hold of enough money to buy the *Bugle*, here. I had only four thousand dollars; and the price was six thousand. One of the *Chronicle* boys happened to speak about it in the composing room. Denny heard him. And he came to look me up. A pawnbroker uncle of his, on Chatham Square, had died and left him an enormous fortune of something like $2,100. Denny had delusions of grandeur. He wanted to be a great editor with a mahogany office, and to have senators and governors send in their cards to him.

"He thought this would be a good start — though I tried to explain to him it wouldn't. So he begged me to let him buy a third interest in the *Bugle*, and come out here and help me make it a second *Chronicle*. I am the *Bugle*'s editorial and reportorial staff. Denny Blayne is the composing-and-job-room force and associate business manager. Poor chap! Thus far, there doesn't seem much chance of his getting back his two-thousand-dollar investment. But he's having lots of fun out of it. You see it's the first time he was ever north of Fourteenth Street, in New York. Or out of Manhattan Island, except on Sunday trips to Coney. So it's all a wonderful foreign land to him. He —"

The girl was looking tremulously down at her spoiled and rumpled red hat. Now she broke in on Hildreth's laborious efforts at impersonal talk.

"Brant!" she exclaimed. "You laughed at me when I tried to thank you, and your beautiful dog shook himself free of me. But I owe my life to both of you. And I want —"

"Please!" he begged, profoundly embarrassed. "Please don't! Praise Thane, all you want to. He did a clever and plucky job. But you don't owe *me* anything at all. I came up, as usual, too late to be of any use. I grabbed your tam, and I made a grandstand play at mock-heroics. That was all. Except to wreck the hat and muss your hair. If it hadn't been for Thane, I couldn't have done a thing — not even get here in time for my useless stunt with your red hat."

"I —"

"And Thane doesn't need to be thanked. With the right kind of dog, the helping of humans is all in the day's work. So, shan't we

27

please forget it? You're badly shaken up by the excitement. Hadn't you better go home and rest? I'm going back to look for my fishing things, up there on the ridge. So —"

He made as though to start away. But Kay stopped him.

"Please wait," she said, beginning to gather her scattered paraphernalia of the interrupted morning's sport. "If you're going back to Sark, by way of the ridge, I'll walk back with you. It's shorter, that way, too."

Undecided, he stood glowering at her. Then, with a shrug of resignation he helped her pick up her rod and creel and to gather the five strewn trout that had spilled from the basket. It seemed he was not to be allowed to drop her acquaintance at will and to adhere to his careful resolve to see nothing of her. She had decided otherwise. Without gross rudeness, he could not escape another half-hour in her torturing company.

They set off, side by side, breasting the slope; Thane frisking joyously about them, blithe to be in motion anew.

"I was so glad to hear you had come back here!" she said, as they moved along. "I've been away, since before Easter. I just got home, day before yesterday. Ralph told me you had bought the *Bugle*. He had a copy of it in his study. You've made a wonderful improvement in it, already."

"Yes," agreed Hildreth. "I suppose we have.

28

But that's a rather doubtful compliment. When my mother said the *Bugle* is 'beginning to look up,' Denny Blayne told her: 'Sure it's beginning to look up. It's so flat on its back, it can't look in no other direction.' We found it in a frightful mess. At first glance, it didn't seem so bad. But most of the ads were 'dead ones' — that means advertisements that have been stopped long ago, and that the paper keeps on running to pad its pages and to tempt other advertisers and to look prosperous."

"I see."

"And the type was about half gone and the other half was defaced. The junk-pile linotype machine bogged down at every tenth word. There were a slew of 'dead' subscriptions still running, too; and a lot more that hadn't been paid up in years. Apart from all that and from about nine hundred other handicaps, it was in fine condition. No wonder we got it so cheap! But we aren't licked yet. This isn't a whine, understand. It's a statement of our start, and it's to be compared, some day, with our success."

"Oh, I hope so! It's fine of you to take it so nicely, when you must have been cheated from the very beginning. Ralph said that at first the town didn't think you'd be able to bring out more than two issues of it, with everything against you, as it was. But —"

"It's been a pretty wakeful month or two," he admitted. "We began by weeding out the dead ads and the dead subscriptions, so we'd know where we stood. Then we went deep into the hole for new type and to get the linotype patched up. After that, it was up to us to get out such a good paper that the county people would have to subscribe. When the subscribers begin to pour in, the ads will follow. As a start, we boosted the advertising rates from the old price of ten cents an inch to twenty-two cents an inch (fifty cents, to one-time advertisers). Somehow most of the few advertisers stood for it, when we sang a song of future circulation to them. Of course, the thing that will keep us out of the poorhouse is the county-and-town advertising. There's due to be a lot of that in a little while now, and lots more in the fall. The *Bugle* gets all that, you know. It's our one lifesaver, till we get the paper going as we want it to. . . . But I'm boring you with all this shoptalk. I'm sorry. It —"

"You're not boring me one bit!" she denied. "And — oh, I *do* hope you are going to make a success of it!"

"We are," he answered, simply. "It all depends on the kind of weekly paper we get out. We're making the right start, we think. And we're beginning to get results. Thanks for believing in it and for wishing it luck."

"I do, indeed," she said with a shade more earnestness than the situation seemed to call for. "And you're going to come to see me, often — ever so often — aren't you, and talk it over with me and tell me about your progress? And you'll bring this glorious collie along?"

She paused, as if for the civil or enthusiastic assent she seemed to expect. Instead, there was a moment's embarrassed silence. Kay glanced at the man in surprise. His brow was clouded and his firm lips were set. Then he spoke.

"I'm sorry you asked me to call," said he, "because, surely you must see I can't. The last time I was at your house was almost seven years ago. That evening your brother did me the honor to forbid me to enter it again. I wrote you about it, and you said he had convinced you he was right. So —"

"And I've even forgotten what the silly squabble was about!" she answered. "But surely you aren't going to let a childish quarrel hang on for all this time, Brant? That would be petty. And you never used to be petty. Never except the time I asked you to think of me only as a friend after a spat we had, and you said you would always think of me as a 'friend' with the letter 'r' left out of the word. That wasn't very nice of you, you know, even if it was rather clever. Anyhow, bygones are going to be bygones, and you're coming to see me. *Say* you are."

"It is your brother's house," doggedly insisted Brant. "And it was your brother who ordered me out of it. Until your brother invites me to it again, I can't very well call. I don't want to seem rude or to seem unappreciative. But honestly I don't want to risk another command to keep out. Don't you understand?"

"I understand only that you're being very silly and stubborn. And very much like a man — which is the same thing," she answered, stiffly. "But Ralph *will* ask you to call. I'll see that he does, since you won't be big enough to forget the foolish way he behaved when he wasn't much more than a boy. Does that satisfy your lofty self-respect, fair sir?"

"Thanks," he said, shortly.

His mind was racing ahead to the campaign he had planned against the graft element which ruled Preakness County — to an exposure of the pitiable conditions prevailing in the county almshouse — to the padding of county labor payrolls — to the more than suspected connivance of the authorities with the rumrunning ring — to the scamping of county road jobs, and the like.

All these things were tied up with the present officials of Preakness County, of whom Ralph Cormick was a leader. No, it did not seem likely, once the campaign was launched, that Ralph would ask the *Bugle*'s editor to his house, or encourage his acquaintance with Kay.

For an occult reason that he could not analyze, this forecast was strangely distasteful to Hildreth. So was the knowledge that his seeming boorishness in regard to the girl's invitation must have prejudiced her sharply against him at the very outset of their new friendship — an outset rendered goldenly auspicious by Thane's

32

gaily heroic rescue of her and by his own sensationally plucky deed.

Ashamed of his seeming ungraciousness, he said, more lightly:

"But, in any case, the other half of your invitation can't be accepted. I mean Thane's half of it."

"Why? Did Ralph order *him* away, too?" she asked in bland innocence. "If he did, I shall make him write an apology to the grand dog and invite him to dinner."

"No," laughed Hildreth, "your brother didn't enact the Angel With The Fiery Sword, in Thane's case, and wave him forth from the Cormick Garden of Eden. Thane isn't quite three years old, yet. So he wasn't included in the ban of seven years ago. But my mother says you have a big police dog — Mowgli is his name, isn't it? — at your house. Collies and police dogs don't always get on together like twin turtle doves. I'd hate to turn a neighborly call into a very vehement dogfight. So Thane must stay at home. There! *That* isn't 'silly and stubborn and very much like a man,' is it, Kay? It's just common sense and a regard for your furniture and rugs — which is much more like a woman, isn't it?"

"I had forgotten about Mowgli," answered the girl. "He is a splendid dog. He is a prize winner and he is highly trained, and all that. But somehow, he and I have never gotten to be very good friends. Now, Thane and I have sworn eternal chumship. At least, *I* have. Do you really think he and Mowgli would quarrel?"

"I'm afraid so; and if they did, there'd be all sorts of a rumpus. Why, Thane even snarls through the office window at Sheriff Aschar Coult's great police dog, every time the dog drives past in Coult's car! He —"

"That isn't Aschar Coult's dog," corrected Kay, "that's Mowgli. Sheriff Coult raised him, and he owned him for five years. Then, last fall, he gave him to Ralph. He's a beauty, isn't he? But he still cares more for Aschar Coult than he does for Ralph. He's always trotting up to the Coult place to visit his old master. And Mr. Coult borrows him, sometimes, for a companion on his long business rides from one end of the county to the other. That's how you happened to see him in the sheriff's car. Perhaps we can persuade Mr. Coult to take him on such a ride or keep him at his house, when Thane comes to call."

Chapter IV

"It's queer that Coult would give away a dog he had bred and brought up and trained. Even to a friend like your brother," commented Brant. "Especially if he's still so fond of Mowgli that he borrows him to go on his drives. Most men —"

"There is a deep and dark and horrific scandal connected with that," explained Kay. "Mowgli always went everywhere with Mr. Coult. A reporter for one of the Paterson papers wrote a story about it. He said the sheriff of Preakness County kept a savage police dog to help him track down criminals. The story spread. One Sunday paper told of the pack of man-eating dogs that were kept by Sheriff Coult to kill runaway prisoners and to tear down petty criminals. It was awfully funny. But Mr. Coult was furious to think anyone could believe such a vile thing of him. So he gave Mowgli to Ralph."

"But —"

"After that, he could say on oath that he didn't even own one dog. He's the most sensitive man I ever knew. The papers speak of him always as 'the political boss of Preakness County.' And it riles him. He says he isn't even the boss of his own sheriff job. Because his very best efforts can't stamp out booze-running through the county; and that as fast as he stamps out one nest of moonshiners up yonder in the mountains another one starts in; and because as fast as he raids a speak-easy, two new speak-easies are opened. He gets so discouraged, sometimes! And then the out-of-county papers are forever saying such cruelly unjust things about him. Even the *Bugle* used to, when Clament Mayne ran it. I'm so glad the *Bugle* is in the hands of the right kind of man at last!"

"Yes," agreed Hildreth, absently.

Brant was visualizing this "most sensitive man," Aschar Coult, sheriff of Preakness County and the known power behind every political move in the region. A giant, with shoulders like a steam radiator, and a barrel chest and a woodenly inscrutable face, and a manner which was anything Coult might wish it to be at any chosen moment.

In a locked drawer of his desk at the *Bugle* office, Brant had a sheaf of notes about Sheriff Aschar Coult's recognized or suspected activities, ready for amplification and use as soon as full proof should be forthcoming. Ralph Cormick was known as Coult's right-hand man and chum. Brant had a more than vague suspicion that Coult manipulated the younger and better bred Freeholder chairman's activities quite as completely as a Bergen ever worked a Charlie McCarthy.

"Some day I'm coming to the *Bugle* office, to look over the paper," volunteered Kay. "You ought to be glad I don't insist on writing poems for it. Besides, I want to see this partner of yours, Denny Blayne. He sounds as if he might be a character."

"He is a *rough* pet," warned Hildreth. "He may shock you or disgust you. But he's the salt of the earth. Besides, he's a big incentive to me. Every time I get to feeling we're going to fail, I look at him. And I remember he has put all his cash into our venture, and thrown over his good *Chronicle* job, too — just because he likes me and because he has faith in our future. Then I realize we *can't* fail. We have no right to. I've got to make good, on Denny's account.

"Yes, and on my mother's, too. She is so un-reasonably happy to have me back at home again; and she has such unlimited belief in me! Why, she reads every line of every week's *Bugle* — ads and all — as excitedly as you'd read a new-discovered play of Shakespeare's! It's not funny. It's pathetic. All the same, I've got to justify her foolishly divine faith in her son. Does that sound maudlin?"

"No!" declared Kay, with a little catch in her breath. "It doesn't. And you know it doesn't. It's splendid. And something tells me you're going to make a gorgeous success of it. I am going to get Ralph and Aschar Coult, and every other influential man I know, to root for you and do all they can to help you along."

Even while he thanked her, he could scarcely hide the ironic smile that twisted at his lips as he calculated how much help or even tolerance he must count on from Coult and Cormick and the other "influential men" of the county, when his campaign for decent government should be launched. The averted smile had crept to his lips only, and not to his heart. There was. something inexpressibly sweet in the girl's quick and eager sympathy for his efforts.

Brant was aware of an odd sense of pain as he realized that soon or late she must side either with her brother and his friends or with the man who was exposing their political corruption. He could not doubt which side she would take in such issue. He had found her again, only to lose her. This time, to lose her through his own quixotic efforts to help to cleanse the county his father had built up and his ancestors had founded.

Thus when he parted from her at the gate of the Cormick grounds, Brant walked on to his own office with a new dejection. For the moment, he could feel none of his usual glad battle spirit.

He could remember only that his long struggle to drive from his heart the image of Kay Cormick had been in vain and worse than in vain; and that he was about to antagonize her forever by his attacks on her brother and her closest acquaintances. Sore tempted he was to abandon his long and carefully prepared

38

campaign; and to leave undone his father's work.

Then he drew a deep breath and squared his shoulders and strode faster toward his office, the big collie gamboling about him as he went.

"Thane," muttered the man, "someone said that the Path of Duty is sweet. Thane, Someone is a liar. Just the same, I'm afraid we've got to go ahead and play the game as God gives us light to play it."

The *Bugle* came out, weekly, on Saturday morning; after the drudgelike work of "make-up" on Thursdays and Fridays. Thus, Saturday was a comparatively light day at the office; which was why Hildreth had chosen Saturday morning for his unfulfilled fishing jaunt.

Now, as he neared the office he noted that several passers-by were carrying fresh copies of the newly issued paper in their pockets or hands, and that one or two more had paused to read or glance over it. Yes, already there was interest taken in the *Bugle*. There was fresh life in the sheet and it was making an appeal to local readers. There could be no doubt about that.

Brant had brought to bear on the half-dead *Bugle* the enlivening methods and the experience he had gleaned during his seven years on the great New York daily where he and Denny Blayne had worked. He had adjusted such methods to small-town conditions, with a rare knowledge of news values and of neighborhood interests. His innovations were beginning to bear fruit. If only he could tide over the first year of debt-paying and circulation-building, there might yet be a goodly future for his enterprise.

He entered the three-room, one-story shack which housed the *Bugle*. A squat and swart and gimlet-eyed little man, shirt-sleeved and grease-smeared, lolled back in the editorial chair, a fatuous smile on his sharp face, reading and rereading a single column of the just-published paper. He looked up with a grin, as Brant Hildreth entered the office.

"Well?" he hailed. "Where's all them trout fish? Did you leave 'em for a truck to bring after you? You might have toted just fifty or sixty of 'em along, as samples. Didn't you get any?"

"No," said Brant, shamefacedly. "And I lost my rod and fly book, too. At least, I forgot them, and —"

"Huh!" grunted the other, in utter contempt. "What did I tell you? To think of going out after a mess of fish with nothing but a measly bamboo twig and a thread of a line and some flies that ain't even real flies! A greengoods man, in the good old days, might just as well have used cigar coupons as baits for his suckers. Now, if you'd just done like I said, and dropped a nice swad of dynamite into that brook —"

"Denny!" reproved Hildreth. "If ever you talk in that blasphemous way to any of these chronic trout fishermen around Sark, they'll burn our paper on the church green, and you along with it. To suggest dynamiting a trout brook is as rotten as to —"

"As to bleed the county white with a million fancy kinds of graft, like some of these noble-souled trout fishermen do?" suggested Denny. "Well, maybe yes. Likewise and also, maybe no. Gee, but we sure put out a slick paper, this time! Best yet. I don't want to sling bokays at *me;* but the best thing in the whole sheet is that 'Seen in Sark' column of mine. I was just giving it the twice over, when you came in. Pretty smooth stuff, I'll say. I can't see where any of that Greeley and Dana and Pulitzer and Watterson crowd of editors, that you're always mooing about, had anything on this column of mine. Read it over yet?"

He offered the paper to Hildreth, with modest pride, with the "Seen in Sark" column folded outward.

To humor the little East-sider's voluble pride in the literary effort, Brant took the sheet from him and pretended to glance at it. He felt he had no need to do so. For he had read and re-vised and pruned and softened every item in it, in manuscript, sternly deleting one or two things in which Denny took special pride and whose appearance in print would have caused mortal offense if not libel suit.

Hildreth had yielded to Blayne's entreaties to be allowed to write for the paper. He himself

41

had suggested the weekly "Seen in Sark" column. Denny had come to the rural district from the heart of Manhattan's lower East Side. To him, every sight and every phase of rural life were as starkly new and bewildering as the daily routine of a central Mongolian province would be to the average American. Some of the little chap's comments on what he saw and heard were amusing. Others were startling. The former type of observations, Brant allowed him to incorporate in his cherished weekly column.

These were attracting jocose attention in the neighborhood and were already a popular and looked-for feature of the paper. For example: On the preceding week a hundred farmers and their hired men had laughed themselves sick at the naïve item:

"Solon Grisset drove a fine husky yoke of pinkish-brown oxen past this office, yesterday. He told ye scribe he had just bought them. Well, Solon, they sure are a nice looking brace of oxen, and they're a grand foundation for any new dairy."

Similarly had the local housewives chuckled in delight at an item warning them to beware of the brand of milk sold in that region.

"It can't be healthy for folks, like good New York milk is," the writer had continued. *"Because if you leave this Sark milk standing for only just a few hours, a thick yellowish scum gets to forming all over the top of it."*

The suburban mind reveled in these unconscious exhibitions of clownishness and of city ignorance; even as did the New Yorkers fifty years ago in the stage exaggerations of countrymen coming to the city. The column was becoming the talk of Sark. As a rule it was the first thing turned to by the average reader as soon as the weekly paper was received.

Denny regarded with smug complacency these tributes to his literary genius. For years, he had had to "set up" the work of professional writers, in the *Chronicle* composing room. Now, thanks to his part ownership in a paper, he was privileged to be a writer on his own account.

A name, near the very bottom of the page, caught Hildreth's carelessly wandering eye. He looked more closely at the item containing it. Denny, following the direction of his gaze, explained:

"We was about an inch or two or three shy, at the end of the column. So I just tossed off another one, to make it fit. I meant to show it to you, but I forgot."

Chapter V

Hildreth did not heed the pattering words. He was reading and then with horror, rereading, the unedited paragraph. It ran:

Don't ever say again there isn't any Santy Claus. Because ye scribe knows better. He saw him, only just this morning; slipslopping along Sussex Street like a comic valentine on its hind legs. He has whiskers a mile long and they are snow white except where they're piebald with good eating-tobacco. And he's got an 1840 vintage high hat that looks like maybe it used to be a hen's nest when it was young.

Old? ask we. Ye scribe opines the ancient geezer was a busboy at Belshazzar's Feast.

And he's got a pallbearer coat he most likely pinched when Abraham Lincoln wasn't looking. And his teeth are easy a half-century younger than what he is. They show bad teamwork, too. When he talks, they sound like a lame horse cantering across a covered bridge.

And he's got a Wool Trust wig that E. Booth (actor) would have looked proud in. Only it don't fit so good under his museum vintage hat. And he's about the funniest sight ye scribe ever saw outside a Sunday comic.

And a urchin (boy) told ye scribe the old callariper's name is ex-Senator Derek Groot. And he sure looks it. And Sark is lucky indeed to be the storage warehouse where Santy parks himself between Xmastimes. If this here Groot is a senator, then it must take a flashlight to tell the Senate apart from a mummy foundry, say we.

P. S. We can understand how he may of got all those food spots on the front of his pallbearer coat. But we can't figure how he got them on the back of it.

Brant looked up, thunderstruck, from his second perusal of the scurrilously vulgar thing. It was so unspeakable, so incredible, so vilely brutal that he could not grasp its full significance all at once. Truly, literary endeavor holds pitfalls for the uncurbed beginner. Especially for a beginner who mistakes ridicule for humor!

Denny Blayne beamed down at his partner.

"That's about the best I've done!" he chuckled. "I'm beginning to get the hang of it, all right, all right. Besides, it's a good jolt for the old cuss. As I went past him I tried to be social-like. And I says: 'Howdy, Gramp!' He

45

give me a look, like I was mud — a look with a couple of hard kicks in it — and he potters on, leaving me standing there. So I bears it in mind, and I write something that's a funny crack and at the same time gets back at him. That's the nice thing about this writing game. It gives folks a chance to —"

"Denny!" gasped Hildreth. "Good Lord, man, the village idiot would have had better sense and better taste than to do a rotten thing like this. In the first place, there's no sportsmanship in making fun of people who can't come back at you. In the second, there's nothing funny about ridiculing *any* old person. In the third, Derek Groot is a former United States Senator and he used to be the biggest man between here and Trenton."

"That old — ?"

"Why, my father began life by studying law in Senator Groot's office! And the Senator did a hundred kindnesses for my family. He was like a grandfather to me when I was a kid! He's very old, now, and he's retired from law and from politics, and he dresses as statesmen used to dress in his youth. But that's nothing to laugh at. Everyone in Preakness County reveres him as a demigod — everyone except the few modern grafters who have heard his opinion of them. And even that crowd would as soon think of painting purple whiskers on the bust of Washington in the courthouse, as of guying Senator Groot.

46

"It remained for a rank outsider to do it; and to prejudice every decent-minded man and woman in the county against us and against our paper. We'll lose subscribers by this, and we'll lose our self-respect, too. I'd make a public apology to him, next week; only that would only leave things worse. I'll write him a personal apology this morning though, and —"

"Nope!" contradicted Denny, sour and glum at the reception of his masterpiece. "Nope. I'll do my own apologizing, thanks, when there's any to be done. I'm still thinking that was a dandy good piece I wrote and that you've misjudged it wrong. But if he was a pal of your dad's, I'm sorry I riled you. I'll tell him so, if you like. But —"

"That would make it worse, too," said Brant, gloomily. "I'll write to him, myself. But the mischief is done. Old as he is, he's still the foremost man in the county, when he wants to be. And the decent people take his word as law. If his word is against us, we may as well put up the shutters. But all that is nothing to the way I feel about his having to read such a thing about himself, in the paper his friend's son edits."

"Gee, ain't I said a coupla times that I'm sorry?" snarled Denny Blayne. "Want me to sing it? What's the main idea of rubbing it in? I'm a mile past the age when I'd stand for a lecture from anyone. Lay off'n it, I'm telling you."

Muttering and scowling, he stamped back into the rear room — joint composing and job room — and slammed the flimsy pine door behind him.

Brant stared after the irate little tough in dumb disgust. Before he could pick up the fallen newspaper again, the street door opened. Its doorway was blocked from side to side by the widest shoulders in Preakness County.

Sheriff Aschar Coult came breezily into the editorial room, seeming to dwarf it by his giant bulk. He wore his city-going black suit and the wide-brimmed black hat and string tie which gave him the look of a western statesman of 1890. Up to the editorial desk he swung his leisurely way, one huge hand outthrust in professional good-fellowship. Not seeming to note the unenthusiastic return clasp of his host's fingers, Coult laughed loudly as in appreciation of some rare witticism.

"Great stuff, Hildreth!" he applauded. "It's got us all a-roaring, down at the courthouse. The whole little sheet is blame' good, right along now, for that matter. I hear lots of folks saying so. But that crack about old Senator Groot! Boy, you certainly swing a mean typewriter!"

"But I didn't —"

"There's more than one of us, down there," went on Coult, "who have been itching to take a swat at the pompous old fossil. Only we didn't like to rile the neighbors. You've got grit, Hildreth. I'll say that for you. And we'll see you get a subscriber for every one you lose by lam-

48

basting old Groot. That's a pledge. You're due to lose plenty. But I can get you plenty. We —"

"Thanks," interposed Hildreth, curtly. "But you're wrong about that item being funny. It was abominable. I am going to write and tell the Senator so. He —"

"Huh!" snorted Coult, in high disdain. "Losing your nerve, hey? Backing down? Never do that, Boy! Never hit out till you have weighed what it'll cost. But then keep right on hitting, harder and harder. I gave you credit for more sand than to get scared and apologize. Why, one of the things I dropped in here to say is that my secretary is working, right now, on a rip-roaring funny poem about the old dodo for your next issue. Let it run with no name signed, to it, of course. But it's a scream. I'll send him around here with it as soon as he gets it polished right. Then —"

"You say that's '*one* of the things' you came to see me about," interrupted Brant, sickly discouraged at trying to explain his view of the matter, and seeking to get clear of the wretched topic. "What were the other things? I'm starting out for lunch in a few minutes, and —"

"I won't need five minutes to do my talking," said the sheriff, placidly, as he seated himself in the desk chair and leaned back in it, looking up at his unwelcoming host. "Have a cigar? Nope? Don't blame you. They're election smokes, left over. I'm trying to get rid of them. Now, then, Hildreth, here's the notion in a nutshell: You know the history of this paper, I take it. When you were here before, and long before your time, Old Man Isaacs was content to run it like a good quiet conservative backwoods sheet, and to take his profit from his share of the state and municipal advertising and by treating the right folks right. So much for that."

"Well?" prompted the perplexed Hildreth, as Coult paused to fill a pipe.

"Then that fool nephew of his inherited it," proceeded the sheriff. "Came up here from Pompton Lakes to take hold of it. He had a swad of wild-eyed reform notions and so forth. First crack out of the box, he began to hammer the good old time-honored local institootions and all that buncombe. I warned him Preakness County didn't want a little runt of a muckraker running its only paper. I warned him fair. He wouldn't be warned. (These reformers never will.) So, presently, he went broke; and he got out. And the paper just hobbled along on one leg, with his creditors managing it at long range, till you stepped in and bought it. So much for past history."

He lighted his pipe with meticulous care, then continued:

"The boys like the way you've started out. You're a live wire. We want to do right by you and give you all the good boosting we can. But we want you to do right by us, too, Boy. Understand that. Understand it, good and plenty."

"I'm aiming to do right by everyone, now

and always, Mr. Coult," answered Brant, quietly, choosing his words with visible care. "But most of all I want to do right by Preakness County. If that right-doing should conflict with any other interests here, then so much the worse for the other interests."

"That's pretty talk," approved Coult, nodding. "Only save it for your editorials. Don't waste it behind shut doors. Let's get down to cases. The county and municipal advertising averages around four thousand dollars. This year, it'll be a lot more, what with election and the sheriff-sales and the road bids and all such. And it can be swung to be even more than that, if it's handled the right way. We can do you a whole bushel of good, Boy. Only — it'll have to be understood, good and plain, between you and me, at the start, how the split is going to be made."

"The split?" echoed Brant, innocently.

"Yes, the rake-off. The share we draw down from what we throw your way," said Coult, impatient at such denseness. "We're alone, so we can talk turkey. What's your idea of the size of our slice of your advertising profits? First of all, I know to the penny what we're going to ask and what we mean to get. But I want your ideas, too. That'll give us something to go on. What percentage?"

"You mean," faltered Hildreth, "you mean that, in order to get the county and municipal advertising, as usual, for the *Bugle*, I'll have to

51

give you a rake-off on all of it?"

"And they said you'd been working on a New York paper!" scoffed Coult. "I guess they had you working on the Sunday-school supplement, didn't they? You sure are plenty innocent, Boy. Do you suppose we're out for our health, over there at the courthouse? We've got to eat, haven't we? I told you we'll treat you right. But you've got to treat us right, too. And I'll be on hand to see you do it. Now you'll listen while I tell you the share we're due to draw down from the ads we —"

A jingling crash from beyond the flimsy door of the composing room gave evidence that Denny had spilled a galley of hand type. Coult leaped to his feet, as an animal might spring aside from a trap.

Chapter VI

"It's all right, Denny!" called Hildreth. "I've got enough. Now transcribe your notes on this sweet talk of ours and we'll both swear to it, for next week's paper. That's all, Mr. Coult," he finished, smiling at the purple-visaged sheriff. "I plan to do quite a bit, to wash this county clean; and you've given me a beautiful start. Thanks."

From the editor's benignly smiling face to the noncommittal shut door the sheriff glared for an instant. Then all at once he grew cool again, and his face took on its wonted woodenness of aspect.

"You rat!" he said, with almost a caress in his soft tone. "So that's the trick? Reform stuff, hey? I thought you had more sense. But I see I've got to step on you, just the way I stepped on young Mayne. Only, with you, it won't take so long. I give you a month, at most. Maybe a lot less. I'm going to smash you and your tin-pan paper as easy as my car would run over a sick cat. Now go ahead with the notes your stenographer has been taking. Print them all over the county. Your number is up. And you're on the tobog. One month, at the most."

There was no hint of threat or of bluster in

his even voice nor in his expressionless face. Knocking his pipe on the floor he strolled out of the building.

A second later Denny's head was thrust in through the composing-room doorway.

"Was you calling me?" he asked. "I thought I heard you say, 'Denny'! But I had just dropped a half-dozen 'takes' of type all over the —"

"No," answered Brant. "It's all right. I'll talk to you about it later. I've got some work to do, now."

He sat down at his desk. With use of skilled reportorial memory, he began to write a verbatim account of his interview with Aschar Coult. But, before he had been scribbling for ten minutes the street door opened again.

This time the visitor's meager form did not half fill the entrance; although the crown of his high hat all but brushed the top of the doorsill. Hildreth glanced up from his work, to see a cadaverous and unbelievably old and gaunt figure crossing the room slowly toward him.

The newcomer was clad in a long black frock coat and high collar and white bow tie. His trousers were tight in the calves and his high hat was bell-crowned. A white beard fell almost to his waist. His shining white hair was palpably a wig. But the cameo sharpness of his classic features and the glint of his hot black eyes and an indefinable dignity saved him from any taint of ludicrousness.

He leaned on a malacca cane with a gold

head. His thin old hands were like bird claws. Just now, his black eyes were ablaze. His ashen cheeks were tinged with the ghost of an angry flush. Feebly, yet aggressively, he stumped across the room toward Brant.

Hildreth rose, with hand outstretched, and hurried to greet the caller.

"Senator Groot!" he exclaimed. "This is an honor. I was just going to write to you. Sit down, won't you?"

Groot ignored the welcoming hand and the cordial words. Still leaning on his cane, he groped in his tail pocket and produced a copy of the day's *Bugle*. Pointing with one bony finger to the item concerning himself, he demanded in rage-shaken accusation:

"Are you responsible for this — this indecent squib, Mr. Hildreth?"

"I am responsible for everything in the *Bugle*, Senator," answered Brant. "But there is no excuse for that paragraph; and I was about to write to say so to you and to apologize and explain that it —"

"If you had happened to brush against me, by accident, upon the street," icily commented Groot, "an apology would be in order. For a — a *thing* like this, no apology can suffice. In the days of my youth, I should have called you to the field of honor, to atone for it. In this degenerate age, there is but one method of dealing with a cur. I have come here to apply that method. And to punish you in the only way in a

55

gentleman's power."

As he spoke, he swung aloft the malacca stick he carried. He brought it down with all his force across Brant Hildreth's face. The old man's strength was pitifully fragile. Yet the puny blow raised a weal on Brant's cheek. Hildreth stood stockstill, his hands at his sides, his eyes fixed on the pathetically wrathful old face.

A second time the cane wabbled aloft. But the impetus of its own motion pulled it free from the feeble fingers. To the floor it clattered. Brant stooped down, without a word; picked up the stick and handed it back to the wielder.

Groot was panting and trembling and all but tottering, from his unwontedly violent exertion and excitement. Hildreth thought the old man was about to fall. The bony fingers closed, unconsciously, about the gold head of the cane which Brant thrust back into his hand. Groot leaned heavily upon it to maintain his balance.

Denny Blayne, hearing the office door open, had come out from the composing room. Petrified, he had stood in the threshold and watched the brief scene of castigation. Now, recovering his breath, he surged forward.

"If you've got a greatgrandson at home, friend," he snarled at the pantingly speechless Groot, "or a dozen of 'em, send 'em here. I'll bust 'em into small independent republics, for this! As for that screed you're sore about, I —"

"Shut up, Denny!" ordered Brant. "Open the

56

outer door, will you?"

He put an arm about the tottering and speechless and spent oldster, gently helping him out of the office and to the senator's waiting barouche. Hildreth lifted him tenderly to the seat of it and signaled the coachman to drive home. Then, followed by the sputteringly indignant Denny, he returned to his desk.

"Down t' the *Chronicle*," Blayne was orating, "they told me you boxed four fast rounds with Jack Dempsey, once, for the noospaper; and he couldn't put you out. They said you're a terror, in a scrap. You look it, too. Yet you let that old cimmaron whang you with a stick! It don't make sense to me. You couldn't slug him, maybe, at his age; but you could have —"

The telephone jangled viciously. Brant answered it. Two minutes later, he turned to Blayne.

"It's our paper people, Denny," said he, dazed. "They called up to say they've got to stop our credit; and that we can't get any more paper except for spot cash — which we haven't got. I —"

Again the bell tingled. Again, Hildreth answered the call. Again he turned dazedly to Blayne.

"It's Gowen & Craik," said he. "They're canceling their ad. The only big advertisers we have! . . . No more credit; and our best ad out. Aschar Coult must have worked fast. He's kept the wires buzzing, this past fifteen minutes.

And he's got results. That's more than *we're* due to get, at this rate. Do you realize what all this means, Denny? We're out of cash. We're out of credit. We're out of our best advertisers. This Groot business will cost us a crowd of decent subscribers. We're — we're flat busted, Denny. We're *out!*"

"You're going to turn yellow and quit?" asked Denny, in contempt for the quiver in his partner's voice.

"Quit?" shouted Hildreth, stung to life by the implied slur. "*Quit*, eh? Not in ten thousand years! Now that we've got nothing left to fight with or to fight for — here's where we begin to FIGHT!"

Chapter VII

It is easy to strike a heroic attitude and to de-claim: "Don't give up the ship!" or "I have just begun to fight!" or "My centre is retreating; my wings are crushed; I shall attack!" or any of a dozen other valiant sentiments. It is quite an-other thing to live up to them.

In the first flush of wrath at the collapse of all his resources, Brant Hildreth had shouted his defiance of fate and his resolve to go on fighting. To fulfill his own fierce declaration of war was less easy. Indeed, it seemed a little more than impossible.

The *Bugle* was deep in debt for sorely-needed repairs and for still worse-needed new type and for the patching up of its one linotyping ma-chine and for the goodly quantity of paper bought as a part of the initial equipment. At best, much luck and more brain would have been needed to float the venture until such time as the corner might be turned and Easy Street discovered.

Now the task seemed absurdly hopeless.

Coult could be relied on to find a way to de-flect the municipal and county advertising — which are the heart and lungs and motive power of most rural journals — even as he had caused the canceling of the *Bugle*'s largest commercial advertisement and the withdrawal of credit by the white-paper concern.

Senator Groot's hosts of revering friends and admirers must assuredly take hot offence at the scurrilous insult to the agéd statesman; and stop their subscriptions to the paper which had vilified him. The item had antagonized the decent element of the county — the very element Hildreth had relied on for support in his antigraft campaign. The ring of local politicians would perform prodigies, fairly or foully, to smash the *Bugle* and its luckless editor.

Denny, with the persistent optimism of his class and type, could not share Hildreth's pessimistic ideas. His own East-side fighting blood was pleasantly atingle at prospect of the newly hopeless conflict ahead of him and his partner.

"What's all the gloom for?" he demanded, when Brant undertook to point out to him more fully their misfortune and the dead wall facing them. "We still got the *Bugle*, ain't we? We still know how to print it and how to write it, don't we? We still got the same marks to shoot at that we been collecting ammunition for. We got enough paper to bring out a couple or so editions more. Some of our advertisers ain't quit on us yet."

"But we —"

"That courthouse outfit ain't been able to nail our skins to their barn door — yet. We're still on our hindlegs and we still got the use of our fists and the use of our brains — if any. So what's the crapehanging about? Time enough to squeal and to frame alibis when our seconds drag us out of the ring, feet-forwards. Till then, we're fighting, Bo. And the others is due to know there's been a fight, before they down us."

"You're right," admitted Brant, his thick shoulders squaring. "You're dead right. You're a better sportsman than I am, Denny. Besides, I've sunk every cent of yours in this mess, along with all my own cash. And it's the least I can do — to fight till I'm out. We won't wait to dig up more proofs or hunt for new facts, the way we meant to, before we launch our campaign. It's going to start — and start *big* — in this next issue. Let's get busy. They can crush us. But so they could crush a hornet. It won't be all pie for them. That's one comfort. And —"

"And about this old Groot cuss that I spilled the beans by guying," went on Blayne, fidgeting. "If you say so, I'll go to him and I'll —"

"Let him alone," commanded Hildreth. "That's done. It can't be undone. We'll make the fight, with what we've got left. No use wasting time trying to pick up broken pieces that can't be mended."

During the week, three small advertisers canceled. So did a veritable flurry of new and old subscribers. The mail was swamped by indignant letters, denouncing the affront to the

61

loved old ex-senator. Boys, one night, smashed every window in the little *Bugle* building. Several people who had nodded in neighborly fashion to Brant, on the street, now passed him by with heads averted.

Then, on the next Saturday morning, a figurative bombshell exploded in Preakness County. The *Bugle* came out, as usual; but with most unusual contents. Inside of a half day the edition was exhausted and Denny was sweating to bring out an extra stack of papers.

The keynote of the sensation was struck in the four-column editorial, down the middle of the front page, signed by Hildreth.

Tersely, it set forth the olden glories of town and county and then went on to contrast them with present conditions. The shameful mismanagement of the almshouse, the winking at illicit liquor's manufacture and distribution, the jobbing of road work and other Freeholder activities, the wholesale bribery and graft and election fraud system — these and other abuses were cited tersely yet strongly.

The editorial went on to declare its intention to fight the battle of the clean element of the region; in the exposing and punishment of these outrages. It promised full legal proof, to back all its accusations. It called on the decent folk of Preakness County to stand behind it in this struggle for the county's future and fair name.

On another column of the front page was the

verbatim account — in the form of a sworn affidavit — of Hildreth's conversation with Sheriff Aschar Coult and the latter's demand for graft in the matter of public advertising. This was followed by a statement of Coult's instant reprisal in the way of deflecting advertising and of causing the shutdown of paper credit for the *Bugle*.

Elsewhere, on not only the front page but conspicuously on other pages, were recitals of various cases of maladministration.

Foremost and most dramatically written among these was Brant Hildreth's description of his own recent visit to the almshouse; a tale of its filth and squalor, of the rotting and meager food and shoddily insufficient clothes meted out to the wretched inmates. Brant made a conservative calculation as to the maximum actual cost for such clothing and food and for the other cruelly stinted outlays. He compared the total with that claimed by the Freeholders in their annually published budget statement. The discrepancy was appalling.

Hildreth made of this feature a really fine human interest story, in no way maudlinly sentimental yet profoundly stirring in its vivid picture of the needless hardships inflicted on helpless paupers and old people. He had even unearthed several instances wherein half-sick and wholly unfit paupers had been made to work in road gangs, without payment and as part of their piteous "duty to the institution which fed them"; and how their daily "wages" were added to the county's payroll expenses.

It was one of those revelations which, if false, should land the accusers in prison for criminal libel, and which, if true, should send the guilty officials to the same place.

In addition to the exposures wherewith that issue of the *Bugle* fairly bristled, there were the usual chatty local news and comments; written amusingly and attractively. There was even a new feature on the editorial page, run in a parallel column to Denny Blayne's "Seen in Sark."

This innovation was called "Thane and Other Dogs." It was headed by a short introduction to the effect that every normal man and woman and child is keenly interested in dogs and that a dog column has as rightful a place in any home paper as has a column on any other popular theme.

Then was reprinted Senator Vest's familiar but ever-touching Eulogy on Dogs. Next was an account of Thane's clever driving of the Holstein bull away from a human the brute had attacked (with no hint given as to the human's identity); and a picked up rewritten item of a dog that returned home to its master across nine hundred miles of strange territory. The column ended with a dozen sentences of quaint philosophy, headed:

"Thane Says —:"

Altogether, apart from its sensational charges and from the exposure stories, the issue was the best and newsiest and cleverest thus far printed by the *Bugle*'s new editor. Small wonder that its fame flew through the town and the rural settlements and that the edition was bought up long before nightfall!

In a black-face type box at the top of the front page was a brief appeal, signed by both partners. It said they asked no help and looked for no reward, in devoting their paper to the betterment of Preakness County. But it bade all fair-minded people to note their efforts to do this and to bring out an interesting sheet; and it asked for any merited appreciation and support in the way of advertising and of circulation.

As it turned out, there was no need for such an appeal. Within twenty-four hours, the subscriptions began avalanching in. Whether the subscribers were actuated by a desire to help those who were trying to help the county or whether they merely wished to make certain of grandstand seats for what promised to be a highly diverting battle royal, Brant did not care to know. Enough that more subscriptions were received within three days than had been gleaned before in six weeks.

Local advertisements, small and large, poured into the office, as well. Merchants and others with goods to exploit were swift to recognize the circulation value of such a sensational paper, and to profit by it. Firmly, Hildreth discriminated between these and the few advertisers who had stood by him.

The newcomers — as well as two of the merchants who had withdrawn their ads and who wished to renew — were confronted by a stiff advance of rates. Gulping, they swallowed perforce the disciplinary dose.

Brant and Denny arranged for a doubling of the usual number of copies to be printed, a needful increase which made hideous inroads into their scanty remaining stock of white paper.

Denny was noisily jubilant. Brant Hildreth was taciturn and grimly alert, as becomes a fighter who has landed a lucky punch on a larger opponent and who knows he may expect a drastic return assault.

In the midst of their night-and-day work on the next week's paper, a long legal-looking envelope arrived at the office, addressed to Hildreth. It contained a single large sheet of typewriting — a letter, signed, also in type, "Old Roman." Idly Brant began to glance over the anonymous missive. Presently his initial disgust at anonymity changed to breathless interest.

Tersely, savagely, yet in merciless clearness, the nameless writer sketched certain local political abuses, and gave chapter and verse for his charges of personal and official graft.

It was a masterly document. In a footnote it indicated where and how the *Bugle* might obtain confirmation of the most sweeping of the accusations; and it promised a similar letter the following week, if the present communication should be printed.

Brant Hildreth spent the next twenty-four hours in following the clues supplied by the footnote. At the end of that time he was morally convinced of the charges' truth. Accordingly, "Old Roman's" letter occupied the space, in the next issue, which Brant's editorial had taken, the week before.

In effect, "Old Roman" accused Sheriff Aschar Coult of protecting the illicit liquor traffic. He declared the sheriff masked this protection by organizing fake raids which brought him great credit for zeal and brilliancy, but which really harmed none of the raided lawbreakers.

He gave instance after instance (some of which Brant was able to confirm, during his tour of investigation) wherein arrested and raided speak-easy owners had been permitted to start operations again, at once, or where the evidence against them had vanished by the time they came to trial. Not one genuine conviction and adequate punishment had Coult scored against any of them, despite his spectacular crusades.

This was the chief indictment in the anonymous letter. Other phases of it were scarcely less damning.

Who the writer could be, Hildreth was not able to guess. Someone of education, of course; and someone of keen legal acumen and of uncanny knowledge of the seamy side of county politics. Possibly, as Brant reflected, a disgruntled member of the ring who sought thus to pay a grudge against his confederates.

In any event, it was tremendous campaign material for the *Bugle*.

Chapter VIII

The partners made special arrangements with the C. G. and X. spur railroad. They had also many volunteer newsboys for the distributing of this forthcoming bumper issue of their paper. At seven o'clock on Saturday morning, some of the still-warm bundles of *Bugles* were given to the boys. Others were carried by Denny to the railroad station.

By nine o'clock, Brant learned of the first concrete blow struck by the courthouse ring, in the battle. All week there had been no word or other sign from the attacked politicians. Aschar Coult had even nodded pleasantly to Hildreth when, twice, he chanced to meet the editor on the street.

But, before the partners had finished breakfast on this Saturday morning, tidings of disaster began to pour in. The newsboys had been assailed and beaten up by seemingly drunken thugs, as they set forth on their routes. Their stock of papers had been wrenched from them and had been torn or burned or otherwise rendered unreadable.

Worse — through some apparent misunderstanding of orders, the train baggageman had neglected to toss the bundles off at the various local station platforms, through the county's stretch of rail line; and had carried the entire lot all the way to the junction, undistributed. There, by a similar misunderstanding of directions, the stacks of papers had been shunted onto a main-line express train; and, by this time, were well on their way toward Chicago.

In short, the whole edition had been wiped out, except for the sixty-odd copies which were deliverable by mail.

For six hours, stripped to the waist, Brant and Denny wrought in their stuffy composing-and-pressrooms. At the end of that time a new edition was ready to go forth — an edition whose front page display type box told the tale of the other edition's fate at the hands of the courthouse gang and its satellites.

In hired cars, Brant and Denny made personal distribution of these new papers, from end to end of the county's rural region, while two members of the New Jersey State Police — to whose commandant Hildreth had telephoned his predicament — guarded the group of scared boys who were double paid to distribute the *Bugle* to subscribers in and around Sark.

On an impromptu newsstand, nailed up in front of the newspaper's office and protected by a third state trooper, piles of *Bugles* were on sale. A husky hired man — the gruff man-of-all-work who had been for the past twelve years in the employ of Hildreth's mother — acted as salesman here. With a club tucked under his arm he handed out papers and made change for hundreds of curiosity seekers who thronged to buy the all-but-missing edition.

The day was saved — or, rather, the night; for it was well past midnight before the work was accomplished and the full issue in circulation. Worn out, but happy, Blayne and Hildreth went to bed; and slept the clock around. They had won the initial skirmish in their grimly hopeless warfare. But it had well-nigh drained their dwindling resources.

Ever since the outset of his hammer-and-tongs campaign, Hildreth had lived in a subconscious dread of meeting Kay Cormick again. In so small a community it was inevitable they should come face to face, at almost any time. Brant told himself she would either cut him or avoid in some other way the meeting.

For, long before now, Aschar Coult and her brother must have succeeded in prejudicing her most bitterly against him; in painting him as a blend of blackguard and fanatic. He had attacked them and their institutions, mercilessly. Kay herself was part of the regime he was assailing. Hence, he could hope for little save detestation from her.

Through the thick of his exciting work, Hildreth had been contemptuously vexed at his inability to put Kay out of his thoughts. Ever she seeped back to his mind, and ever with that same strange pang of longing and of loss. That he was indirectly fighting her, in fighting her brother and her friends, robbed the conflict of any battle joy; and made it a miserable task for him. In vain he strove to dismiss the whole theme from his consciousness. Always it stole back to him, obsessing and compelling.

Then, in the middle of the week following the ring's effort to destroy the *Bugle*'s whole edition, the inevitable happened. On his way home from the office, Brant all but collided with a woman who was coming out of a Main Street shop. He stepped back with a mumbled apology for his awkwardness.

The apology broke in the middle as he recognized the woman as Kay Cormick.

Hildreth lifted his hat and stepped stiffly to one side to let Kay pass by. But the girl would not have it so. Instead, she stopped short, laughing mockingly up into his glum face.

"Oh, Brant, how *silly* you are!" she exclaimed in amused reproach. "You were actually going to stalk away in gloomy dignity and not even say 'Hello'! How unutterably babyish and cranky of you! Aren't you just a little ashamed of yourself for behaving so? *Say* you are!" she demanded imperiously.

"You bet I am!" declared Brant with vehemence, as a ton weight lifted itself from his heart. "Horribly and hopefully ashamed! But — But —"

"But you were foolish enough to think I would carry on a deadly Capulet-Montague feud with you — just because you are shooting popgun corks at my brother and at established customs here? Brant, you must be taking yourself terribly seriously if you think a little thing like that would break up our friendship. Why haven't you been to see me?"

The man stood blankly astounded at the unforeseen turn the dreaded meeting had taken. But in his heart he was illogically happy. Then he found tongue.

"I was afraid you'd never want to speak to me again!" he blurted with awkward boyishness. "I didn't see how you could. I am doing my best to put your brother and his friends — they're your own friends, too — out of business. I was afraid you'd be so loyal to them that you'd —"

"That I'd make faces at you on the street, or go around the block to keep from meeting you?" she supplemented. "Oh, Brant, for a grown man you're hopelessly absurd! Why, even if the *Bugle*'s ridiculous attacks could do us any harm — even if the preposterous charges it makes against us were true — why should you and I stop being friends?"

"You're wonderful!" he exclaimed, a shade of hoarseness in his voice. "Oh, Kay, you're — you're *great!*"

Into her big eyes crept a momentary softness, making them luminous and wondrous tender. Then, as with a sharp effort, she returned to matter-of-factness in look and tone.

"It was nonsense for you to worry about it at all," she told him reprovingly. "You might have known better — ever and ever so much better, Brant. Why, even if we weren't old-time chums, you and I, could I be stiff and horrid with you after what happened out at the trout stream? You tried to throw away your life for me that day. It was magnificent of you, and —"

"Now it's Miss Kay Cormick who is talking nonsense," he broke in, fidgetily embarrassed at her praise. "I didn't do a thing — except get there too late to be of use. It was Thane that turned the trick. And even Thane didn't do it as a hero stunt. It was a lark to him. You saw that. He had a beautiful time. He —"

"Did you know he could keep the bull busy and that I wasn't in any danger?" she demanded. "Did you know that all the time?"

"Well, you see, he had never worked cattle before," said Hildreth. "So I couldn't be sure. I could only hope he —"

"You 'could only hope'?" she insisted. "That isn't true. You did more. A million times more. When nothing but that dog was between me and a frightful kind of mangling — and when you weren't sure Thane could save me — what did you do? You got between me and the bull and you ran at him waving my scarlet hat; to draw him away from me and make him attack you. There aren't any words to say 'Thank you' in, for a thing like that, Brant. And I'm not

74

going to make you any redder and more uncomfortable by trying to. But when you remember what you did out there, you — you ought to be slapped and stood in a corner for thinking I wouldn't speak to you. Now do you understand?"

"Yes," he made answer, his voice muffled, his breath fast, "now I understand. And I'm going to ask a big favor of you, Kay. You seem to have a distorted idea that you're in my debt for the useless grandstand play I made, with your red hat. You aren't. But if you want to square the imaginary debt forever, you can do it by promising to forget all about what I did — or rather what I didn't — and stop being grateful to me."

"But I —"

"I hate to have people grateful to me," he persisted. "Soon or late it makes them bored. Gratitude is mighty wearying, for both parties. Besides — I'd rather have you drop my acquaintance than be friends with me only because you have a false idea that you're in my debt. I don't mean that to be ungracious, but —"

"I know," she replied, softly. "But you and I were friends, seven years ago, Brant. And I want us always to be. Gratitude has nothing to do with it. Now, when are you and Thane coming to see us?"

"Us?"

"Ralph and me. To talk over old times and —"

She broke off, abruptly, in her invitation, as she noted the unbidden cloud which settled on his face, wiping out the boyish eagerness of his expression and making him look suddenly old and careworn.

Chapter IX

"There!" she accused. "You're getting ready to say you won't enter our house till Ralph asks you to! Well, Ralph will. I'll tell him to tonight when he gets home from court. I'll have him salve your tender feelings by writing you a charmingly cordial note, inviting you and Thane to dinner and promising that Mowgli shall either be locked up in his yard or else sent to Aschar Coult's for the night. Now does *that* appease your Mightiness's self-esteem? If not —"

A scurrying corn-colored mass of fur whizzed up to her, dancing excitedly around her feet and seeking to lure her into noticing it. Thane had accompanied Hildreth, as usual, on the walk from office to house. A half-block back, the collie had stopped to touch noses with a tiny street mongrel; and to romp gently with the friendly little crossbreed.

The latter's owner had come out of a store and whistled to his puppy. Whereupon, Thane had jogged onward to rejoin his master. Then it was that the dog saw and recognized the girl he had rescued from the entertainingly murderous Holstein.

Kay stooped to pat him. She rumpled his

silky ears, crooning at him in a high voice, which pleased the collie, vastly.

"That's queer!" commented Brant. "Thane isn't given to effusiveness, except with me. I never saw him offer to make friends like this with a stranger."

"Thane and I aren't strangers," she denied, her hand resting caressingly on the collie's head. "He knows what he saved me from, and it makes him fond of me. We're always fonder, aren't we, of people we do big things for, than of people who do big things for us? Thane and I are chums already. Besides, I've been reading his column in the *Bugle*. The *'Thane Says'* column. It's fine."

"Thanks."

"If only his master could be induced to write the same way, and stop trying to be a martyr-like reformer, the *Bugle* would be the best country paper in America."

"It —"

"Why not think over that suggestion, Brant?" she finished, laughingly, yet with an undernote of earnestness in her sweet voice. "When we used to read about Don Quixote going about tilting with windmills and redressing wrongs that never existed and proclaiming himself the champion of causes that needed no champion — other people used to think the story was funny. But to me, it always seemed terribly pathetic."

"It was."

"Just as it seems to me, now, when you come back here to sweet old Preakness County and announce that it is full of sin and corruption and that it is your mission to purify it. Where's your sense of humor, Brant? Can't you see how preposterous and absurd it all is?"

"I can see how clean and decent I'm trying to make it," he evaded. "And now that I know you aren't hurt or angry at what I'm doing, I can tackle the sorry job with a lighter heart and a stronger arm. So —"

"By the way, who is 'Old Roman'? Ralph says he'd give anything to find out. Those 'Old Roman' letters are what he and Aschar Coult are most furious at, in the whole paper. They say you, personally, couldn't know about the things he attacks; and that the letters aren't written in your style, either. So they wonder who —"

She broke off with a little cry of surprise. She had been standing with one hand still resting on Thane's head. Now, from beyond the two talkers came a vicious snarl. A yellow-gray body flashed forward, hurling itself at the collie.

Thane wheeled, just in time to avoid a flank attack. He and a big German police dog clashed, chest to chest, rearing and snapping.

"Mowgli!" called Kay, sharply.

The police dog paid no heed to her command. He continued to tear away at the mattress of hair which formed so baffling an armor for Thane's neck and shoulders.

The young collie had not sought the fray. But, thus assailed, he gave no inch of ground. In gay ferocity he returned the heavier dog's onslaught. One of his curved eyeteeth scored Mowgli's cheek, deeply, and slashed the ear.

Before the fight could go further, a hamlike hand reached out and caught the snarling police dog by the collar; lifting him high in air, with as much ease as though the eighty-pound dog were a kitten. The collar was of brass-studded morocco leather; wide and thick. It stood the strain of the sudden access of weight, as Mowgli was jerked from his feet.

In the same instant, Brant called imperatively to Thane. Obedient, though reluctant to leave the just-begun fight, the collie turned, almost in mid-air, and stepped back to his master's side. His instant move enabled him to miss a fervid kick aimed at him by Aschar Coult, who had borne down upon the incipient warfare and who still held big Mowgli dangling and struggling in the air.

A younger and more slender man came running up, as the combatants were parted.

Coult and Ralph Cormick had been driving home from Paterson, in Coult's car; Mowgli seated in the rumble. At sight of Kay standing in public, chatting with Brant Hildreth, the sheriff instinctively had slowed his car almost to a standstill. Mowgli had taken advantage of the slackened speed to leap out of the rumble and fling himself at the unoffending collie.

Even in the excitement of the instant, Kay found time for an approving glance at Thane; in admiration of the collie's immediate and perfect obedience, and contrasting it with the forceful measures needed to remove Mowgli from the encounter. Then she turned to her brother.

"Mowgli was the aggressor," she said. "Thane only defended himself. But he did it beautifully. Ralph, you remember Brant Hildreth? I was just asking him to dine with us some evening soon. I told him you'd write and ask him. It will be good to talk over old times together, we three. He —"

Again, she broke off in her speech; the glad smile fading into worry as she noted her brother's reception of what she was saying. At mention of his own name, Brant had stepped forward and held out his hand. There was noticeable dearth of enthusiasm in his action, but it was wholly civil.

Ralph Cormick eyed the proffered hand as though it were a peculiarly unlovely specimen of snail or leech. With his own hands at his sides, he ignored the hotly flushing Brant, and addressed Kay.

"It will not be convenient to have Mr. Hildreth at my house," said he. "I hope he won't need a stronger hint that I want no communication of any kind between him and my family. If you're on your way home, Kay, we'll give you a lift."

He turned away, toward the car. But his sister would not have it so.

"Ralph!" she exclaimed in vexed dismay. "*Ralph!* Have you gone crazy, and lost the last trace of your breeding? Brant," she went on, with eager apology, "I'm sorrier and more ashamed than I can say. But the house is as much mine as it is Ralph's. And I ask you again please to overlook my brother's boorishness, and come to see me. Won't you? *Say* you will!"

Brant's fingers gripped hers in quick appreciation. Then he dropped her little hand and said gravely:

"Thank you. Thanks, a million times. And you're not to worry yourself over Cormick's behavior to me. I knew what to expect. It doesn't bother me. Thanks, again — and goodby."

Raising his hat, he set off homeward. The big young corn-colored collie followed at his master's heels, yet ever glancing truculently back at the hard-held police dog.

Half a block farther on, hurrying footsteps behind him made Hildreth turn to see who was following so fast. Aschar Coult fell into step with him, having sent Mowgli back in the car with the sulking Ralph and Cormick's indignant sister.

"Hildreth," began Coult, with no preamble, "that was a grand good stunt of yours, in blocking us by a hurry-up edition in place of the one we — the one that got accidentally junked. I'll hand you that. I'm enough of a born scrapper to appreciate a good punch — even when I'm the punch*ee*. But it won't work, another time. It —"

"It won't have to," returned Hildreth. "I got in touch with the president of the C. G. and X. road, and he's having an investigation made. He's given me his pledge, as a man and a Mason — and he'll keep it — that no more bundles of my papers will be tampered with on the trains or shunted off at the wrong place. The troopers will see the local newsboys don't get mishandled again, too. So —"

"There's more ways of killing a cat than by choking it with radium," philosophized Coult, cryptically; adding: "I'm sorry you've got such a bum idea of my headpiece as to think I'd work the same stunt twice. But let that go. What I was getting at is: You got that edition into circulation, by a real good hustle. Maybe you can circulate the next one. Maybe not. But you're down at the end of your pile. You're at the bottom of the barrel. Your paper supply is pretty near gone; and your cash is about gone, too. You're coming up groggy for the last round, while we're not even puffing. We've got you where we want you. It isn't a question of more'n a month longer for you, at most. Likely, not half as long as that. You're gone."

"We're not."

"Now that that's agreed on, here's my proposition: We've been talking it over, at the courthouse, some of us. We've agreed the *Bugle* is too nice a sheet to throw into the discard. It ought to be kept running, for the good of the county. But you hadn't ought to be kept running it, and making toadpie of everything. At the same time, we don't want you to lose all the cash you put into it, if you'll listen to reason. What did the paper cost you and your partner? Somewhere around six thousand, wasn't it?"

"Yes," answered Brant, his heart beating so fast that his voice sounded muffled and meek. "Yes. Six thousand. Then a lot for repairs, and —"

"And you're still in debt for that," finished Coult. "Now here's our proposition: We're willing to buy the *Bugle* off'n you — lock, stock and barrel — assuming its debts, too. What do you say?"

Chapter X

Brant walked on a few steps without replying. From the corner of his eye he could see an aspect of genuine concern steal across the big man's wooden face, as Coult awaited the answer. Then Hildreth asked, half-humbly, half-craftily:

"What would you folks be willing to pay me for it? It's cost us all we had; and we've made a better paper of it than ever it was before. We won't throw it away for a song, I can tell you. It's a twenty-five per cent better property than it was the day we bought it, and —"

"Good!" interrupted Coult. "That gives us something to go on. You paid six thousand. You claim it's worth twenty-five per cent more than that today. According to that, you must figure it's worth about seven thousand five hundred. Well, suppose we give you a certified check for seventy-five hundred dollars and agree to take over the paper's debts — how does that strike you? No notes, mind you. Spot cash. You've invested six thousand dollars between you; and inside of four months you make a twenty-five per cent turnover. Not so bad. There's only one condition — only one string to it: We gotta know who 'Old Roman' is. That's only fair, isn't it? Now, what do you say?"

"Let me get this thing straight," replied Brant, his voice still muffled, his manner almost fawning. "Do I understand that you and your friends will pay Blayne and myself seventy-five hundred dollars, cash, for the *Bugle*, as it stands; and that you'll take over the paper's indebtedness, too? Is that a bona fide offer?"

"I'm not given to making funny jokes," Coult reassured him. "That's the offer; and it's on the level. Only — remember, you'll have to tell us who 'Old Roman' is; and tell us straight. Now what do you say?"

The fawning meekness fell from Brant Hildreth, as a garment. He threw back his head and laughed with unfeigned merriment. Coult eyed him in sour amaze.

"What do I say?" mocked Hildreth. "What do I *say?* I say you're as stupid a crook as ever I ran across, Aschar Coult, my friend. And they told me you had brains! You must have left all your poor muddled wits at home today. Don't you see what you've done? At first, I didn't dare hope for such good luck. So I let you go on to the end. I —"

"Say!" began Coult, roughly. "If —"

"You and your gang have the name of never spending a plugged nickel, if you can help it, Mr. Sheriff, unless it's the county's money. And then you only spend it on yourselves. *You're* the most cautious spendthrift of the lot. And yet

86

you make me a bona fide offer of seventy-five hundred dollars for a paper that you think is going on the rocks inside of a month at most. If you waited till then, you could get it for a song. But, to shut me up, right off, you're willing to slip seventy-five hundred dollars into my pocket."

"Put in any way you like," said Coult, groping for a clue to the other's wildly exultant talk. "You've heard my offer. It —"

"Yes, I've heard it, Coult!" gaily admitted Hildreth. "And in the next issue of the *Bugle*, all the county's going to hear it. They're going to hear I've got the courthouse gang so scared that you're willing to pay seventy-five hundred dollars to muzzle me. Everyone knows your stinginess. Everyone will know you must be frightened stiff of the *Bugle*, before you'd pay that much hush money. I must have cut you deeper than I knew. I —"

"You poor fool! I'm only aiming to do a good turn for an old neighbor's son!" exploded Coult. "Anyone who knows me —"

"Half an hour ago," rejoiced Brant, "I was sick discouraged. I figured I was fighting a losing battle. Except that you'd tried to scrap an issue of the paper, I couldn't see that I had dented you crooks anywhere! Man, you've given me new heart. I'm winning. *Winning!* I've got you all on the run. I've gotten you to the last ditch — to the place where you'll try to save yourselves by throwing away thousands of dollars to get quit of the pummeling I've given you. Coult, you've made me mighty happy! I —"

"I have?" queried the sheriff, suddenly ice cool and seeming to exhale a queer ophidian deadliness. "Keep on thinking so, Boy. If you're happy, I don't grudge it to you. For you aren't due for overmuch more of it. The crowd were for roughhouse methods, to abate you."

"Yes? If —"

"But me, I'm always for the gentle way of doing things. So long as they can be done gentle. That's why I talked them around to buying you. If you can't be bought, you can be busted. And busted you'll be. That's a promise. Not a threat. Now chase on home and do some more hurrahing. Your hurrah muscles are liable to get rusted from disuse, before long. That's all. I've tried *my* way. Now I'll try the other men's way . . . I'm kind of sorry, too. For, if you weren't plumb crazy, you'd be a good deal of a man, Hildreth."

He turned back; leaving Brant to continue his homeward stroll alone with Thane. With his own departure, the sheriff somehow took much of the momentary exhilaration he had aroused in Hildreth.

Brant knew and knew well that drastic methods would be instituted at once, now that bribery had failed. The enemy would stop fighting with squirt guns and would bring up heavy artillery. If Hildreth was worth wasting seventy-five hundred dollars on as a silencer, he was worth grinding into the earth by less lawful and peaceable means.

Yet, not for more than a minute or two could Hildreth concentrate on the formless danger ahead. Ever into his troubled mind drifted Kay Cormick's face and voice. Ever he reddened at memory of her brother's icy affront to him in her dear presence.

At the office, that afternoon, Brant wrote out, almost word for word, his talk with Aschar Coult and the latter's offer to buy the *Bugle*. Then Hildreth fell to remembering Coult's insistence on knowing the name of "Old Roman," and what Kay had said of Coult's and Ralph's fury at the anonymous attacks in the "Old Roman" letters.

Very evidently they shared Brant's suspicion that one of their own gang was paying off a grudge by playing informer. Vainly, Hildreth mused as to the unknown's identity. Most of the county grafters were either semi-illiterate or of only rudimentary education. Yet these anonymous missives were models of style and of invective. Assuredly, no down-at-heel corrupt rural politician had the brain or the education to fashion them.

A new "Old Roman" letter, containing still further revelations of county maladministration, had arrived by the afternoon mail. Brant read and reread it, puzzled, as he ran over in his mind the few local men who could by any possibility have written it.

Denny came in, while Brant was still reading the typed sheet. In a few words, Hildreth told him of the proposition Coult had made and of the sheriff's ensuing threat. As he listened, Denny lost the worried pucker between his black brows. A grin of rapt inspiration began to wreathe his unshaven little face.

"You figger he'll try to break up our distribution again, this week, Brant?" he asked, as Hildreth finished his recital. "You figger he'll be able to do it? You figger he'll wind up by making us shut the shop? You figger that all them golden and gorjus hopes of ours has got to be folded up and laid away somewheres, like the pants of a dear dead friend? You figger — ?"

"I'm afraid so," said Brant. "Coult is due to get busy along some tougher way than he did last week. Because his dander is up, and because he knows the paper will run an account of the way be tried to buy us. All we can do is to block him, the best we can and as long as we can."

"Nope," denied Denny Blayne, the grin spreading. "Nope. Nope. You're wrong there. That ain't anywheres near all we can do. I got an idee. A reg'lar ol' he-one. It'll block him; and it'll be the biggest ad for the *Bugle* that ever happened. Want me to spill it for you?"

With no vast interest and with no optimism at all, Hildreth nodded, and settled back to listen civilly to something crassly impractical and fantastic.

But, in less than a minute, he was on his feet, agog with enthusiasm. Fantastic the little man's idea most assuredly was. But it was in no way impossible. Brant could see therein a marvelous form of advertising the *Bugle*, by word of mouth, from one end of the county to the other.

"Remember Spike Dougan?" began Denny. "The guy down in the pressroom, at the *Chronicle*, that you went to the front for with Magistrate Daile, when Spike was up for sending his bum brother-in-law to the hospital with a smashed jaw, for swearing at Spike's old mother? You got him off with a reprimand, you'll remember, when it looked like he'd do ninety days at the Island and pay a fine, besides. Spike is a grateful cuss. He ain't like most of us, that way. And he's always been grateful to me for helping him out with the rent money, that time he was fired from the *Chronicle*; and him and his mother was going to be evicted."

"Yes. I remember him. But —"

"Well, last week, I get a letter from him. Whatye s'pose Spike has rose to, this past three years? He's no less than manager for that garage down to Newark where they keep the armored trucks that payrolls are carried in. I'm going to take a half day off and run down to see Spike. If he's got an armored truck that he can spare, we sure can use it."

His jaw jutting out, and his face grotesquely distorted by the ever-expanding grin, Denny Blayne proceeded to unfold his "idee," to a constantly increasing eager interest on the part of his hearer.

At sunrise, on the next Saturday, a fairish crowd stood on the curb, facing the *Bugle* office. Rumors were afloat that the courthouse gang were planning another attempt to prevent the issue's circulation. An hour later, the crowd had swelled to most creditable proportions. Someone pointed down the quiet street, and shouted.

A truly forbidding and formidable object was approaching. It resolved itself, presently, into a huge battleship-gray armored truck, with sinister black muzzles protruding from various loopholes. It drew to a clanking halt in front of the *Bugle*'s office. Then it was seen that four flaring placards in red lettering adorned the truck's exterior.

In large type thereon the thrilled spectators read that the editors of the *Bugle* had reason to fear another strong-arm attempt on the part of Coult and his satellites to destroy or otherwise suppress the issuance of the paper. Wherefore, said the placards, it had been deemed necessary to avert such an outrage by dint of counter-force.

So this armored truck had been chartered for the purpose of distributing the paper to its subscribers in all sections of the county. Thus, the loyal readers of the *Bugle* would not be deprived of their weekly newssheet; and the courthouse gang would not be able to avert the circulating of the articles and editorials which exposed their corrupt methods.

Now, as Hildreth and Denny well knew, there was no more actual need for the hiring of an armored truck to distribute the issue of the *Bugle* than to wear a gas mask in lighting a lawn fire of dead leaves. But both men had been swift to see the splendid advertising value of such a ruse.

Nor had they misjudged its attractions. Thick and thicker the crowd pressed around, scanning the placards and eying with delighted awe the plate armor and the protruding muzzles of the hidden machine guns. All of them had read of armored trucks. Few had seen them.

Chapter XI

An Associated Press reporter, notified in advance by Hildreth, was on hand, avidly taking in every detail of the truck, and watching a line of boys carry out bundles of the newly born *Bugle* and dump them into the dim interior of the warlike vehicle. This was real news. By night, a terse account of it would be in a hundred newspaper offices. The fame of the *Bugle* would be spread, thus, all over the land; as well as mention of its editors' fight against local grafters and strong-arm politicians.

Off trundled the truck on its mission of countywide distribution. Again the impromptu newsstand, presided over by Mrs. Hildreth's surly hired man, was set up on the sidewalk in front of the office, and was piled high with copies of the paper. In almost no time the pile had to be renewed. Everyone was buying *Bugles*. Everyone was reading, excitedly. The newsstand did a whirlwind business for hours.

Brant Hildreth sat back, weary from his all-night work, as he watched the heaps of copies disappear from the stand outside his office door. Denny had gone forth in the truck as super-cargo. Brant was alone. He and Blayne had calculated roughly how long the trip ought to take. When the returning truck was almost due, Brant locked the office and walked up to the courthouse square to meet it.

There were a goodly number of people flocking the square. Word had gone around that the truck would soon be back from its intimidating trip. Those who had not seen it earlier in the day were waiting for a glimpse of it. Also, the Saturday baseball game was just ended. A thousand or so of its spectators debouched from the ball field into the square. They lingered there to see the truck.

On the courthouse steps stood Sheriff Aschar Coult, surrounded by a half-dozen deputies. He was talking earnestly with Ralph Cormick; and with John O'Roon, the tubby little mayor of Sark. The mayor was a pudgy and round-faced bald man with a scar on one cheek and with a perpetual smile which was not pretty to look upon. He resembled a dropsical cherub with grave-robbing proclivities.

At the far side of the square an old-fashioned barouche drew to a standstill. On its box sat an antiquated negro in livery. In the rear seat was former United States Senator Groot. Apparently, the old man was returning through the square from his stately afternoon drive. When he noted the unwonted crowd he had ordered the carriage halted while he should learn the reason for it. Brant Hildreth took a step toward him, from across the square, then hesitated.

What good could it do for him to go and pay his respects to the ancient statesman who had made such pitiful effort to cane him? Derek Groot sat hunched into a semicircle. His mouth worked mechanically, as he chewed the mysterious cud of senility. His chin was on his crossed hands which, in turn, rested on the gold head of his malacca stick. His bell-crowned high hat was pulled far forward above his old black eyes.

Then there was a general shift of attention to something proceeding toward the square from the south end of town. Into sight hove the grim gray armored truck; with its four machine gun barrels glowing black and polished in the sunset. Toward the courthouse it rumbled, on its way to the *Bugle* office. Dour and menacing, it rolled forward.

As it approached the stretch of highway directly in front of the courthouse, Aschar Coult went into action. For this, apparently, he had been waiting.

Followed by the mayor and by the Sark police chief and by its four uniformed policemen and by a brace of deputy sheriffs, he strode forth into the middle of the street, in the path of the oncoming truck. Majestically he raised his hamlike right hand, signaling the armored vehicle to stop.

The crowd pressed close around the truck and around the sheriff and his followers. There was a hush of tense expectancy. The vehicle came to a halt within three feet of where Aschar Coult's gigantic figure and mandatory hand barred its progress.

Like some monstrous gray beetle with shiny black antennae, the truck stood in the sunset light, the crowd packing around it. The inky muzzles of the four machine guns seemed to menace the whole peaceful afternoon world.

Coult's wooden face was as threatening as the guns. He confronted Denny Blayne who had hopped nimbly out of the portable fort and came toward him.

"Well, Mr. Fourflush Sheriff!" hailed Denny. "What's the big idee in stopping us? We're kind of in a hurry to get home."

"You are Dennis Blayne?" demanded Coult, in his best tone of authority, and raising his bull-like voice for all to hear.

"Why, y-y-e-s," confessed Denny. "Now that I come to think it over, it seems I am. My mother used to call me 'Denny.' But that was because she'd known me so long. *Mister* Blayne to *you*, Aschar. But how you guessed my name is beyond me. You sheriffs sure have gimlet brains. There ain't nothing a poor common cuss can hide from you. The —"

"You are Brant Hildreth," continued Coult, addressing Brant who had made his way through the crowd to Blayne's side.

"Don't go denying it, Brant!" implored Denny. "Don't! Maybe he's only bluffing when he says we're Brant Hildreth and Dennis

97

Blayne. But then again, maybe he knows. It's safer to come through clean, when we're up against such a Sherlock Holmes. Let's own up who we are. It'd be bound to come out, some-time, anyhow. He sure is —"

"Brant Hildreth and Dennis Blayne," continued the sheriff, outwardly ignoring Denny's clumsy badinage and a resultant snicker or two from the crowd, "you are under arrest. I charge you with carrying (or causing to be carried) and displaying deadly weapons, in public, as expressly forbidden by the criminal laws of this county and state."

"Brant," whined Denny, reprovingly, "I warned you what'd happen if you kept on car-rying that turrible deadly pencil sharpener in your pocket. Now we're both due to go to jail for life on account of it. At least, Mr. Sheriff," he continued, "I *s'pose* it's on account of his pencil sharpener? That's the only deadly weapon we own, between us; since I lost my penknife last week, through a hole in my pants pocket. But we don't take turns carrying it, and it ain't one of our partnership assets. So what's the sense of arresting me along with him? He —"

Again a snicker from several points in the crowd greeted the little man's buffoonery. Coult's wooden face purpled. But he kept tight hold on his official self-control.

"You are both my prisoners," he continued, in stilted diction, as though reciting a lesson.

"You are under arrest, for illegally carrying and displaying lethal weapons; for the purpose of intimidation."

"What weapons are you talking about, Mr. Coult?" asked Hildreth, signing Denny to silence. "Since we are put to the public humiliation of arrest on a criminal charge, it is our right to be told publicly to what weapons you refer. I will waive any possible rights, as will Blayne, by submitting to search, here and now. You will find I haven't even got the pencil sharpener with me. I left it on my desk. And I am certain Blayne is unarmed. Please search us."

Coult's huge hand waved aside Brant's words as though they had been summer flies that sought to pester him. Still with tight hold on his self-control, the sheriff pointed to the armored truck whose driver had dismounted and was coming forward. Touching with an accusatory forefinger the gleaming black muzzle of the nearest gun, Coult declaimed:

"I refer to the four machine guns with which your truck is equipped. Those guns," he went on, raising his voice still further and letting an oratorical note creep into it, "those four machine guns are carried and displayed by you in defiance of the law and as a threat. Why, one volley from them would fill this square with hundreds of dead and dying!" he finished, with dramatic vehemence.

There was a slight involuntary backward

surge of the crowd from the direct range of the four sinister muzzles. There was a murmur of angry disapproval of the two partners, as folk visualized what might happen were the fearsome engines of death turned loose.

Hitherto, the armored truck incident had provoked pleasant and applauding excitement in the crowd. Now, there was a swirl of revulsion at the menace and potential destruction which Brant and Denny had thus displayed toward their neighbors.

Swift to avail himself of the gust of disapprobation, Aschar Coult rose to higher flights of eloquence.

"One turn of the lever of any one of those four guns," he thundered, "would send a stream of leaden death tearing through this assemblage. Sark has no place and no welcome for men who will threaten such damnable injury to its citizens. I am doing not only my duty as sheriff of Preakness County but as a decent private citizen as well, in placing you both under arrest and in seeing you have no further opportunity to molest my fellow townsmen. I herewith sequestrate this truck, too, including its four engines of destruction, which —"

He got no further. To emphasize his climax, as well as to prove his own fearlessness in face of danger, he had grasped one of the shining black muzzles and given it a punitive tug.

The gun muzzle responded to this sharp

yanking, by coming out of its loophole to a distance of perhaps thirty inches. Coult let go of it, hastily, and stepped back. He was not an expert in the workings of machine guns. But it did not seem natural to him that the barrel should come away from the rest of the gun at a mere pull of a human hand.

Evidently he had destroyed some rather precarious balance. For, as he released his hold on the muzzle, the gun barrel continued to slide slowly outward from its port. Presently, the muzzle end began to outweigh the other part. The barrel slid outward, fast and faster; while Coult and the crowd gaped foolishly.

Then it overbalanced, and tumbled out into the road.

There it lay — the machine gun's barrel, that tube through which, presumably, death-dealing bullets could be made to pour with the speed of summer rain and with the wholesale murderousness of lightning bolts. Harmless and moveless it lay in the road, alongside the truck; while all stared open-mouthed at it.

It was perhaps six feet long and a little more than an inch in diameter. The muzzle, for about three feet, was a gleaming black. The rear half of the barrel was a dull gray, and ended in a screw socket. The awed silence was split by a half-hysterical yell from a plumber in the forefront of the crowd.

"It's — it's a *gas pipe!*" he bellowed.

Sadly, Denny Blayne trotted from one to another of the remaining three gun muzzles, and hauled them out onto the ground. Each and everyone was a six-foot gas pipe, with one end painted black.

The truth hit the whole mob of spectators at practically the same time. From the crowd arose a veritable howl of laughter, an unquenchable and many-keyed explosion of raucous merriment. Men laughed till the tears poured forth. They rocked to and fro and grabbed one another for support.

Their mirth arose cacklingly toward high heaven. It sounded more hideous than the hiss of snakes, in the ear of Aschar Coult, sheriff of Preakness County. Through it his fancy could hear the tolling of his own official knell.

He had hit upon a clever scheme for disgusting and horrifying the county's people with these two strangers who were exposing his comfortable methods of gaining wealth. If the public could be made to look upon Brant and Denny as dangerous to the community by reason of their display of armed force in a peaceful region — if the two could be convicted by Coult's own fellow-ringster-judge and could be fined and imprisoned — their newspaper would collapse during their absence. Public sentiment would set forever against them. Their crusade would be in ruins.

And now, after his carefully staged arrest scene and his thundered accusations —

The crowd continued to shake and reel with

laughter. In their mirth was not a little hysteria, bred of the revulsion and the fear stirred up by Coult's word picture of the damage the horrible guns might have inflicted upon them.

Chapter XII

Brant let the laughing go on, for a time; along with the derisive shafts of rustic wit wherewith members of the throng began to pepper the empurpled and half-apoplectic sheriff.

Hildreth listened, as to divine music. He had denounced the man who misruled Preakness County. Folk had read and had commented and had argued. But, for the most part, they were content to read and to comment and to argue. The public at large is not roused easily to active measures. It might have taken months for the *Bugle* to achieve its ends, along that line.

But, in a single minute, he and Denny had succeeded in making Coult and the courthouse gang supremely ridiculous. They had made the sheriff a public laughingstock — a county joke. This tale would be told and retold, for ten years to come.

When once a leader has been heartily and derisively laughed at by his own constituents — when once he has been changed from hero or villain into an unwilling clown — from that instant his mysterious quality of leadership is gone. Hildreth's newspaper experience had taught him that one wholesale guffaw can wreck a public man's career far more swiftly and utterly than can years of vitriolic denunciation or proofs of wrongdoing. He knew what had just been accomplished, as well as Aschar Coult knew it.

Presently Brant raised his hand for silence. The noise died down. Folk craned their necks, curious and avid to hear the next lines in this sidesplitting comedy.

"Mr. Sheriff," said Hildreth, his pleasant voice carrying far, "I plead guilty, as does my partner — guilty of putting four painted gas pipes through loopholes in a pastworthy and condemned armored truck. (If you will send a deputy inside the truck, to search, he will find there are no deadlier weapons in there than the tool kit and the jack.) Blayne and I confess to 'displaying and causing to be carried' four six-foot lengths of common gas pipe, and we are ready to go along with you as your prisoners. We will go quietly, so you will not need the handcuffs I see dangling from your belt. Shall we start?"

He took a step toward the wing of the courthouse which served as county jail. Again that multiple guffaw rent the air. Again flew the volleys of homemade wit, buzzing about Coult's ears; with maddening assurance that he was forever knocked from his pedestal in the hearts and imaginations of the people who had elected him and before whom he was planning to present himself, that autumn, for re-election.

His thin lips tight-set, the sheriff turned on his heel and shouldered roughly a way for himself through the guying crowd toward the sanctuary of his own private office in the courthouse. Nonplused and confusedly furious, Mayor O'Roon and the deputy sheriffs followed.

The chief of police loudly ordered his constables to clear the square. Tears of laughter still daubing their cheeks, the patrolmen set about their duty. The people dispersed, good-naturedly. The fun was over, anyhow.

The only groups of any considerable size which did not obey at once the mandate of "Move on, now, you!" were those which gathered and continued to gather around Brant Hildreth and Denny, wringing their hands and thumping them on the back in an access of merry gratitude for the best laugh bred in Preakness County during the past ten years.

Through the congratulations, Brant read an undertone of earnestness — of newborn liking and faith. It is in public human nature to seek a leader. One leader had just been overthrown. Unconsciously, the people were groping already for another.

By instinct they were pressing around Brant Hildreth, who had destroyed the hero worship or villain-fear they had felt for Coult and his fellow looters.

When at last Hildreth and Denny were alone in the office of the *Bugle*, and their volunteer escorts had drifted away, down the street, the partners, by tacit consent, gripped each others' hands in a wordless fervor of happiness.

Then, very solemnly and grotesquely, accompanied to his own off-key whistling, Denny Blayne proceeded to execute an improvised Victory Dance all over the outer office. Thane was delighted and thrilled by such spectacular antics. He pranced around the dancer, barking at the top of his lungs and, at every third step, tripping up the inspired performer.

"Shut up, you!" shouted Denny to the dog, as the little man narrowly escaped a bad fall when Thane charged afresh between his twinkling feet. "Say, Brant, what does he want to go barking for when I'm whistling? He —"

"What do you want to go whistling for, when he's barking?" retorted Hildreth, from the creaky depths of the desk chair into which he had thrown himself.

"Now, then," he continued, "if you're quite sure you've got all the excess enthusiasm out of your system, sit down. There are things to be talked over."

"There sure are!" exulted Denny, squatting precariously on a table corner. "Say, I could jaw for a solid year about that stunt of ours! Fire away!"

"We've won another round of the finish fight against a combination that is still liable to clean us out," said Brant, soberly. "That's the only net result of our spree. We've advertised the

Bugle, everywhere. We've gotten out our edition safely, once more. We've made people laugh themselves sick at Aschar Coult and his gang, instead of worshiping them or living in terror of them."

"We sure have! We —"

"That's the entire asset side of the day's happenings. Nothing more. The rest of the situation is just about where it was. Except that Coult will hardly stop, even at murder, now, to get back at us; if I know anything of human nature and of Coult-nature. Most people would sooner be kicked than laughed at. Coult and his ring are going to be a stirred-up hornet's nest, from now on, as far as we're concerned."

"But Coult —"

"Coult's a wise man; a crafty man. He knows his only hope, now, is to get us out of the way and then try to make people forget they guyed him — or else show them it isn't safe to make a laughingstock of Aschar Coult. He'll use you and me as horrible examples of what happens to men who play jokes on him. He —"

"Say!" interrupted Denny, wholly uninterested, and incapable of dragging his mind from the egregious events of the afternoon. "I forgot to tell you. Did you happen to notice Joe Scarry sitting in his car, at the courthouse curb? He was driving through, when he struck the jam of folks and had to stop. He was taking it all in. And he was asking questions, too. D'you know what that means? Scarry's the upstate correspondent for five of the biggest Noo York and Noo Jersey papers. He'll write the story of this. The way he knows how to write it. And that means it'll be a peach. And he'll send it to all of his papers, and they'll print it, full. Guess that's bad, hey? Oh, it's a wow! We —"

"Thane," said Brant, chirping to the big collie that sprawled at his feet, "except for me, you seem to be the only sane creature in this office, just now. So I'll pass along your share of the warning to you. You scrapped with Cormick's police dog, Mowgli, today. You slashed him, too. Not enough to give him a respect for you or to scare him. But enough to make him hate you worse than ever; and to tackle you every time he sees you. Don't crow over the cut you gave him, in the second or two before we stopped the fight. Just be on your guard against him, Thane. Even if Denny hasn't the wit to take in my warning of what's in store for him and me. He thinks we've won a victory, Thane. Well, we haven't. We've scored one small point in a million point game, and we haven't the punch to score an other. Now, both of you run on; while I write the story of this one point we scored. I want to do it while it's still fresh. Chase!"

For another few days there was utter silence and dearth of action from Coult and his courthouse satellites. Once, on Sussex Street, Brant happened to meet the sheriff and Ralph Cormick. The latter spat ostentatiously, in the gutter, and walked past the editor with averted face. But Aschar Coult nodded affably to the man who had made him ridiculous, and tossed a friendly: "Good morning, neighbor!" to him.

Hildreth continued his walk, in no way cheered by the chance meeting. He would have felt more at ease if the sheriff had emulated Cormick's display of scornful aversion. When a man like Coult greeted an avowed enemy thus cordially, it boded no good for the latter, as Brant knew. Thus might a pugilist, cocksure of his own easy ultimate victory, grin pleasantly across the ring, between rounds, at his panting opponent.

Subscriptions were continuing to come in at an incredible speed. New advertisers, not only from Sark, but from all over Preakness County, and even from distant Paterson and Pompton Lakes and Butler, were meeting the increased rates of the *Bugle*. For the moment, it was the best small-town advertising medium in the state. A fairish quantity of white paper, too, had been secured, and negotiations were opened with a mill in New England for a regular supply.

Denny crowed ecstatically over these signs of bright prosperity. But Brant did not crow. More and more, he had a compelling intuition that the trouble he and Blayne had weathered was as nothing compared to that in store for them.

On Wednesday evening, Hildreth came back

to the office, after supper, as usually he did, and settled down to three hours of work at his desk. Since the smashing of the *Bugle* windows, a few weeks earlier, Denny Blayne had insisted on rigging up a cot in the pressroom and sleeping there every night, on guard against possible repetition of the sabotage. Tonight, Denny was out on one of the fast three-mile tramps he took every evening to keep him in condition after his day's work.

As Brant bent over his desk, scribbling furiously and oblivious of his surroundings, Thane started up from a nap at his master's feet. Growling, he dashed toward the front door.

Hildreth glanced around in time to see the door burst open. Two hideous and misshapen figures lurched into the room. There was something unearthly, terrifying, in their aspect and their sensational inrush from the pitch-black night outside.

Brant sprang to his feet. An involuntary cry burst from his lips as he recognized the larger of the two intruders. With a snarl, Thane flung himself at them.

Chapter XIII

A strange and right unwinsome reek filled the small room; brought in with the two shapeless creatures who had broken upon Brant Hildreth's solitude. It was the rankly sickish smell of stagnant water and of decaying vegetation and of river mud. A running pool of muddy water surrounded the pair, as they came to a halt, at Thane's impetuous charge.

One of the two cried out, sharply, to the leaping collie. In blank astonishment, Thane checked his attack, almost in mid-air, and crouched back on his haunches. The voice was as familiar to Brant as to the dog.

"Denny!" gasped Hildreth, incredulously.

The larger of the two newcomers was half-carrying, half-supporting the smaller. Both were coated, inches thick, with brown mud from which draggled irregular festoons of lily pads and other aquatic plants.

Blayne lifted the lesser figure to the office table, dislodging an avalanche of exchanges and books to make room for the body. Then he turned upon Brant, speaking thickly and exuding muddy water from his mouth corners.

"Don't stand gawping there!" ordered Blayne.

"Hop to the phone. Call up Doc Vreeland. One-five-nine is his number. Ask him to get here in a rush. I don't know yet how bad drowned she is."

"She?" echoed Hildreth, picking up the telephone.

"Yep," said Denny over his shoulder as he stretched the mud-disguised body face downward on the table, amid a sea of liquid mud, and began vehemently to apply first aid for the drowning. "I was coming back here. I'd taken the short cut from Gusepple. I was coming to the bridge, next block where the crick joins the pond. I saw a girl in front of me, leaning over the bridge rail. Just as I caught sight of her, there in the dark, she lets out a kind of a holler — or maybe it was a prayer — and over the rail she jumps, spang down into the pond."

"A suicide?"

"Nope," sneered Denny, hard at work on his first-aid efforts. "Just jumped in to see was the water wet, of course, you poor sap. Well, over she goes. And over I go after her. Reg'lar movie stuff — Yep, ask Doc Vreeland to hustle. One-five-nine. Oh, you get his house, at last? Good! — Yep, reg'lar movie stuff, it was. But it's only when I'm halfway betwixt the bridge and the pond below that I happen to remember I've never learned to swim a stroke, and that the pond is maybe a mile deep."

"At the Durkin Lane bridge? It isn't six feet deep, anywhere, there. It's nothing but a soft

113

mudhole, this time of year."

"Uh-huh? Is that so? Now you speak of it, I seem to remember there was just a splash or two of mud somewheres around the bottom of it. I scrambled and wallered and plunged in it for about eight months, till one of my hands happened to hit her shoulder. I got a good hold on her — she was pretty near suffocated by that time and so was I — and I wallered for the bank. In a couple of years more I had got us to solid ground. By that time I guess the whole pond was solid ground. Her and me, between us, had collected all the mud and water out of it. This was the nearest place to bring her, till Doc Vreeland could get to work on her. So here we are. We smell grand, don't we? And we look worse'n we smell. And we feel worse'n we look. But the poor kid seems to be getting her breath and coming to life a little bit. She —"

A convulsive sobbing from the victim of his first-aid ministrations gave evidence that she was far less near to drowning than he had thought. She pushed free from his manipulating hands; and turned and sat up, dazedly, on the table edge.

Then it was that Brant and Denny got their first good view of her. She was a girl of perhaps sixteen, not ill-looking through her streaks of mud. Her clothes, too, before they had been ruined by immersion in the dirty pond, must have been neat and well-cut. She groped blindly for her handkerchief. Denny thrust the

114

office towel into her fumbling fingers. With it she fell to mopping her face and to gouging the mud from her tear-swollen eyes.

"Lie down again," said Brant soothingly. "Dr. Vreeland will be here in a minute or so. Don't try to talk or move. You're all right, till he gets here. Just rest, and —"

"Why did you jump in after me?" demanded the girl, fiercely, as she glared at the astounded Denny. "*Why* did you? If it hadn't been for you, everything would be all over by this time. Now, it's all got to be done again. And — and I may not be brave enough, another time to — to —"

"Hush!" soothed Hildreth. "You mustn't talk. And you mustn't get excited. Just lie still, till Vreeland gets here."

This as the child's hysterical words were lost in a flood of sobs. Brant and Denny looked at each other in silent conjecture. For a moment the room was still, except for the convulsive weeping of the drenched and muddy girl. Then Denny Blayne spoke.

"Don't cry, kid!" he adjured, his rough voice wondrous gentle. "Whatever's happened, it ain't bad enough to be worth killing yourself for. There's a whole swad of bad things that can happen to folks in this bum old world. But not a one of 'em, and not the whole passel of 'em, is worth sooiciding for. Take the word of a guy who knows the game, on that, kid. Nothing's worth it. And there's nothing that can't be cured. It's a quitter's cowardly and plumb crazy way to try to end a trouble. By bumping himself off to some place where he'll sure be in a worse fix than he is now, and where there ain't any cure. Keep on remembering that. Besides, at your age, you can't be a failure or a wreck, even if you try to. Too many cards is still left in the pack. There's too much time ahead of you. Luck's always waiting for you, just ahead. Buck up!"

The sobs were growing fainter. Denny spoke again.

"Besides," he said, "there's a little gold croocifix hanging to that chain around your neck. That means you and your folks believes the same things *I* believe in. Gawd has set a time for you and me to stay here. And a time for us to come home to Him. If you go changing His schedules, like you just tried to — well, that's pretty near as wicked as it's foolish. And it's like horning into a house at three o'clock in the afternoon when you've been asked to a party there at eight that night. You can't count on much of a glad hand when you show up five hours before you're expected or wanted. If —"

The front door opened again, this time to admit the hastily summoned physician.

Half an hour later, Dr. Vreeland drove the resuscitated girl to her parents' home, in his own car. By that time, too, the partners had learned her name and her story.

She was one Greta Melvin, daughter of the superintendent of the local hard rubber works. Her narrative was infinitely more silly than sordid. Her plight was the direct result of snobbery. Not of sin.

Pruned of its sobs and hesitancies and repetitions, her recital to Dr. Vreeland had the elements of cynic humor rather than of potential tragedy. She was in her second year at the Sark High School. The fraternity system had been introduced at the school, two or three years earlier. "Fraternities" was the generic term used there, for fraternity and sorority and mixed clubs as well. These various societies had become hidebound little cliques of varying snobbishness. Non-members were regarded more or less as social pariahs.

Greta Melvin, for some reason, had not been "rushed" for any of these secret organizations; nor had her best efforts succeeded in winning for her a membership in even the least exclusive of them. Stung with a morbid sense of disgrace and failure, the foolish child had sought to escape the supposed shame and unpopularity by drowning herself.

Yes, it was absurd. But it was not the first nor the fiftieth time that a similar thing has happened; as the news reports of the past few years will attest. Somehow, it roused Brant Hildreth to red-hot indignation.

Chapter XIV

Scarce had the front door closed on the doctor and the repentantly nerve-shaken girl when Hildreth sat again at his desk, shoving aside the half-finished editorial he had been writing, and working feverishly on a new theme. Here Denny found him when the little chap emerged, clean and re-clad, from the inner room whither he had gone to clear away the effects of his immersion.

"Listen, Denny!" Brant hailed him, excitedly. "We've got a side-line crusade to wage, along with our regular campaign. I've read a lot about these school secret societies; but it never came home to me, till just now. Man, they're hotbeds of snobbery, nearly all of them! This is supposed to be a free land, where everyone has an equal chance."

"Says *you!*"

"So we send our children to school. To learn there that if you don't belong to the right crowd you're an outcast. They make snobbishness a fine art. They leave school and go out into the big world with a fixed idea that they must get in with a set that looks down on its neighbors. Woodrow Wilson smashed the secret society system at Princeton, on just those grounds. I'm going to smash it at Sark."

"More power to you!" applauded Blayne. "While you're about it, smash the thing a coupla hard ones, for *me*. If it keeps on, I'm liable to grow web feet from prowling through the mud, looking for kids that can't get elected to some slick s'ciety. Go to it!"

"I wouldn't bring in this Melvin child's name, if I could help it," continued Brant. "Though the crusade would be no good, unless I could pin it to some local happening, as an example of what the societies can lead to. But Dr. Vreeland called up the chief of police, to make inquiries about it, while his car was coming for him. So he must stop at Police Headquarters on the way home, to explain and to keep them from arresting the poor youngster. That means her name is going on the blotter and that everyone in Sark will know about it by tomorrow. So, we can't do her any harm or get her any worse publicity by trying to make her case an illustration of the rottenness of the school secret society system. I'm working on it, now. Tomorrow, I am going to get an interview with the president of the Sark Board of Education and with Dr. Betts and with the county's school commissioners. The poor crazy little girl! Denny, you were a good bit of a man to jump in after her, like that, when you don't even know how to swim. I —"

"Sure I was!" assented Denny. "And if I'd had a second to think it over, she'd be down there in the mud, this minute. It's a funny thing about sooicide — If you try it and fail, they arrest you. If you try it and succeed, the law can't do a thing to you . . . I was hoping maybe you'd let me write something about it for my 'Seen in Sark' column. How about it? 'Wednesday night an obscure but handsome young hero — Heaven's Answer to the Maiden's Prayer, as you might well call him — rescued from several tons of mud a heroine in distress. Asked about his magnificent exploit, Mr. D. Blayne said with becoming modesty that he'd like to bat the block off the liar who circulated the idee that mud baths are ben'ficial. Mr. Blayne says he knows different.' How's that?"

The next issue of the *Bugle* — which was brought out and distributed without interference and without the aid of an armored truck — contained a scorching editorial assailing the school secret society; as an institution in general and as applied to Sark in particular. There were satisfactorily disapproving statements in another column, from local and county school heads. Brant, in a front-page spread, had told simply yet with tremendous effectiveness the pitiful story of Greta Melvin.

At last, he seemed to have hit upon a line of crusade which the public at large endorsed and which even the courthouse gang did not oppose. There was neither graft nor prestige in the societies, whereby the ring could profit. Wherefore they hailed with relief a grievance which might help to shift a trifle of denunciation from themselves.

They needed such relief, sorely. For the same issue of the *Bugle* contained a diverting account of Aschar Coult's attempt to disarm a gas-pipe equipped truck and to arrest its lessees on the charge of carrying murderous weapons. The description was a joy to all but Coult and his satellites, and it revived merrily the laughter of the preceding week.

"Old Roman's" letter was by far the strongest and most mercilessly scathing indictment he thus far had written. Brant was half-afraid to print it, unsoftened; the more so since he must take the writer's word for several of the facts he dwelt on. But, instinctively, he had grown to trust the unknown contributor. There was an undisguisable ring of truth and of assured proof, in everything he wrote.

Such statements as Brant had been able to investigate, in earlier articles, had proven wholly true. Wherefore, taking what he felt to be a negligible chance, he printed the vitriolic article, word for word, as it was written.

The *Bugle* was on the streets of Sark, by nine in the morning. Before eleven, Brant had a caller whose advent gave him an illogical sense of added sunshine and ozone in his somewhat stuffy editorial office, and at sight of whom he sprang from his chair and hurried forward with

121

both hands eagerly outstretched.

"Kay!" he exclaimed. "Oh, this is gorgeous! I never dared hope you'd pay me an editorial call. Sit in my desk chair, won't you? It's safe, as long as you don't lean back too far. There's a broken spring that lets one down, if you do. I'll dump the papers off this visitor's chair, if you'd rather —"

Belatedly he noted what, in his burst of boyish delight and surprise at her advent, he had overlooked, namely, that she returned his effusive greeting with none of the winsome friendliness of a few days agone. Indeed, she was all but curt in her salutation. There was unconcealed vexation in her bronzed little face.

"What's wrong?" he asked, as she seated herself in the proffered desk chair and turned to face him. "You look as if everything had gone crooked today. Can I help?"

"It's you who have made things 'go crooked,' Brant," she told him. "That's why I'm here. You ought to be shaken and then stood in a corner. You're the original Bad Boy of journalism. I wish I could take your paper away from you, before you do any more mischief with it."

"So does your brother," Hildreth reminded her, drily. "And so does his chum, the (more or less) Honorable Aschar Coult. So do numbers of their friends. All of them think that way. All of them wish they could take the *Bugle* away from me. But somehow none of them have managed to do it, yet. . . . Still, if my campaign against them has made *you* sore, I'm horribly sorry. From the way you spoke about it the other day I thought you didn't —"

"Oh, I'm not talking of your silly political tempest-in-a-teapot!" she set him right, impatiently. "That doesn't make me angry, and apparently it doesn't hurt anyone at all — except perhaps the Recording Angel who has to take notes on the language Aschar Coult and Ralph use about you. I'm talking of something that seems likely to do *real* harm."

"What?"

"I'm talking about this idiotic broadside you've fired today, into the school fraternities. It's a bit like stalking for sparrows with a siege gun, isn't it? Isn't it rather small game, for a grown man to try to get the county all stirred up and indignant over a few harmless little high school secret societies? Personally, I think it's rather despicable. That's why I'm here."

"I don't think anything is 'small game' that teaches some children snobbishness and gives needless heartaches to other children," he defended himself. "And most certainly there's nothing petty about an attempted suicide."

"Nonsense!" she disclaimed. "Greta Melvin is a stupid over-sensitive youngster, who is trying to pose as a martyr. If she hadn't been unhappy about being barred from the secret societies, she'd have been unhappy over something else. And to use that as an excuse to abolish all

123

the fraternities at Sark High School, just as I had gotten them nicely organized —"

"You?"

"Certainly. Didn't you know that? When I got back home from college, three years ago, not a soul here had ever thought of such a thing as a fraternity or a sorority or any kind of secret organization, for our school. I had made a regular study of it, at college. It was the theme of my graduation thesis. I had interviewed dozens of authorities. I understood how the societies ought to be formed and conducted, to give the greatest good in every way. So I introduced the system, here at Sark. From the first, it went over, splendidly. We've achieved perfectly remarkable results —"

"Yes," assented Brant, "Denny Blayne fished one of those 'remarkable results' out of the pond hole, the other evening, barely in time to keep from expanding a mere 'result' into a funeral."

"Nonsense!"

"Honestly, Kay, I didn't know you were interested in these societies. But even if I had known, I'm afraid the evil is too big to be allowed to go on. The more I inquire into it, the more I find it has disrupted the American spirit of equality and squareness that we try to inculcate in all our elementary and high schools. It turns the whole student body into sharply divided classes; the 'ins' and the unlucky 'outs.' Greta Melvin was only one of many 'outs' whose feelings were ripped to pieces that way, and whose parents had begun to hold grudges against the parents of luckier pupils who were 'ins.' It has started more than one nasty neighborhood squabble, here and everywhere else. It's time the whole thing was squashed out of existence. And it *is* going to be squashed out of existence, if I can do it. Practically everyone in the county seems to be with me in this."

"It's just wretched neighborhood jealousy," insisted Kay. "Why, I could tell you no end of cases where friendly rivalry among the societies has stimulated study and athletics and —"

"And snobbishness?" supplied Brant, as she hesitated. "Well, if we can't stimulate interest in study and in athletics and all that, without also setting up models of snobbery and causing wholesale heartaches, then the School Board is in a bad way."

"Oh, you're impossible!" fumed Kay.

"So are the societies."

"I might have known there'd be no use appealing to your sense of fairness or to your friendship for me!" she blazed, stung by his pleasant certainty. "I might have known a professional reformer would have no sense of justice. I —"

"Kay!"

"I've stood up for you, ever since you came back here," she continued, a note of pleading in her voice. "I've stood up for you and I've been your stanch friend. You know that. We've been friends, you and I, ever since I was a child. I do think the very least you can do for me is to grant this one simple favor I'm asking you. It means so much to me, Brant! Why, the success of our school societies, here, has been my chief pride. I felt I had accomplished at least one good thing for the town I love. Their success was my success. And now you are trying to destroy it all! It isn't fair, Brant. For my sake, won't —"

"For your sake, I'd do more than I've any right to say and more than you'd have any wish to hear," he answered, sorely disturbed. "You know that. A woman always knows. But an editor isn't just a mere man. He's the guiding wheel of his community, if he amounts to anything. He has no more right to betray what he knows to be the best interests of his town than he'd have the right to betray his country. That sounds cheap and melodramatic, perhaps. But it's the truth. I know these school societies have done a lot of harm. They are likely to do more, if they are allowed to go on. They must be closed down. If you'll let yourself think it over, calmly and sanely and logically, you'll agree with me. I hate, worse than I can tell you, to refuse you any favor in the world. It's like pulling teeth. But —"

"I think, if you don't mind, I won't wait for the rest of the sermon," interposed the girl, hot with vexation and chagrin at her failure and at the impending ruin of her pet school project.

126

"I'm rather in a hurry. I am sorry to have taken up so much of the precious time you might have been spending in launching some new reform for the misfortune of Sark. Good morning."

"Oh, hold on!" cried Hildreth, seeking to stay her haughty progress toward the street. "Hold on, *please!* You're surely not going to walk out on me like that? You're not going to let a squabble over a bunch of school kids interfere with — ?"

"With our friendship?" she hazarded, pausing for an instant, at the door. "No. Of course not. Nothing can interfere with what has ceased to exist. Goodby."

Too hurt and dumbfounded to realize that she had spoken with the same blind impatience which makes a sharply unhappy child slap its loved playmate, Brant Hildreth stared blankly after her receding figure as Kay made her rigid way up the street and from his range of vision.

Chapter XV

Hildreth had scant intimate knowledge of women in general or in particular. Thus he believed in Kay's hasty declaration that their sweet old-time friendship was at an end. He did not take into account that she had always had her own way and that her interest in the high school societies was more intense than in any other county matter.

He had tried therefore to talk to her as he might to another man, in arguing against the societies and in setting forth his own editorial position, not realizing that he must have seemed to her merely priggish and pedantic and hopelessly pigheaded.

With a long sigh, he seated himself again at his desk, and resumed the work which, all at once, seemed strangely flat and uninspiring. He was toiling thus when Denny Blayne came back from his round of the county to see that the paper was distributed according to schedule.

"What's the matter?" queried Blayne, observing his partner's glumness. "You look like an accident on its way to happen. Like you'd been wrote by Edgar A. Poe, Esq. Friend Coult been riling you again? Or has some advertiser canceled? I —"

"No," said Brant, wearily, "no. None of those things. I've just been finding out how much bigger Life is than the people who have to live it. And that it's silly to try to get more out of Life than is in it. That's all. How about —"

The furtive opening of the front door checked him. A girl sidled shyly into the room. It was Greta Melvin; still pallid and shaky from her recent mishap. She returned uncertainly the cordial hail of the two men. Then she addressed Denny Blayne, speaking fast and nervously.

"I was waiting for you to come back here," said she. "I've been waiting over at the drugstore. I saw you —"

"Well, now," declared Denny, "that was mighty friendly and neighborly in you, kid. Anything I can do for you? If there is, just spill it, and I'll —"

"No," she denied. "You've done enough for me. This is something I can do for you — and for Mr. Hildreth, too. Both of you."

She glanced apprehensively out of the nearest window.

"If you don't want to be seen," suggested Brant, puzzled, "come into the composing room. Its windows aren't on the street."

He led the way thither, followed by Greta. Denny went along, mildly curious as to what was pending. As soon as they were in the rear room, the girl took up the thread of her errand.

"My brother Karl is the best fighter, anywhere in Preakness County," she began. "If he had wanted to go into the ring, folks say he'd most likely be heavyweight champion, by now. There isn't anybody that dares make him mad."

She paused, having delivered herself of this family tribute in the course of one long breath. Then, drawing another long breath she continued, at the same rapid fire speed:

"Sheriff Coult had Mayor O'Roon send for Karl, last night, on the quiet, to the mayor's house. Here's what he wanted Karl to do, and he said Sheriff Coult would see he didn't get in trouble over it, and that there'd be a hundred dollars in it for him. He says you and Mr. Hildreth always go up the street together, on your way to supper, nights, and you most always take the short cut through Durkin Lane. He says there's generally nobody else in the lane, that time of day or any other time of day."

"Well?" prompted Denny, as need for another inhalation of breath caused a second pause.

"Well," proceeded Greta, "he wanted Karl to be hanging around there, just beyond the bridge, when you and Mr. Hildreth go through the lane on your way to supper tonight. He wanted Karl to pick a quarrel, somehow, with you, and then begin to beat you up, for all he was worth, and —"

"Huh?" grunted Denny, vastly entertained. "Beat who up? *Me?* A rube beat me up? Him

130

and who else? I'm askin' you. Say, kid, did this mayor person say what I'd be doing, while your big brother was — ?"

"What *could* you do?" half-wailed Greta. "He's twice your size. And you don't look so very strong. That's what the mayor told him, too. But that's only half of it. He said that Mr. Hildreth would be certain to try to stop the fight, and that he'd grab hold of Karl or maybe even hit at him, to make him quit thrashing you. The chief of police and two deputies of Mr. Coult's are to be watching. From the other side of those bushes along the pond. That was the time they were to jump out and grab both of you. They would take oath you both hit Karl, and that Karl seemed to be just defending himself from a brutal attack from two men he hadn't even harmed. And it was going to be a case of felonious assault. And Judge Emerson Bogardus was going to fix higher bail than you could pay. And you both were going to be tried. And both of you were going to get long sentences — Mr. Hildreth, especially. He —"

"Sweet scented frame-up, hey?" commented Denny, as Greta's hurrying voice wabbled. "And it would 'a' went through like greased lightning, too. They'd have had three men to take oath to us beating him up, unprovoked-like. It'd have meant six months, anyhow, for the two of us. But, 'cuse me for jawing, kid, while you was talking to us. You say Big Brother Karl got that job sawed off onto him. Is

131

he going to take it?"

"No," replied Greta. "He isn't. That's the trouble. I was in bed, when he got back from the mayor's last night. I heard him telling Dad about it. Karl said he supposed he'd gotten in bad with all the Coult ring, now, because he had turned down the offer. He said he wasn't going to slug you, after the way you saved me from — from —"

"From getting your clothes still worse muddied up?" supplemented Denny, hastily. "That was the worst you would have got. Just a little more mud on your clothes. Forget it. But I'm thanking your brother for —"

"Dad said he was right to refuse," affirmed Greta. "He said he'd never have spoken to him again if he'd played such a low trick on you, after what you did for me. Dad thinks you're wonderful, Mr. Blayne," she finished, timidly.

"Yep," said Denny, very ill at ease. "He came around here and spilled a lot of thanks on me. So did your ma. Thanks that I didn't want, nor yet deserve. I told them so. They —"

"But that isn't all of it, yet," resumed Greta, on the strength of a new store of breath. "When I was washing the breakfast dishes this morning, Karl came home from downtown. And he went to where Dad was in the woodshed waiting for a carpenter he'd sent for. They didn't know I heard. Karl said he'd just had an inside tip that Mr. Coult had gotten hold of Mart Goebel. When Karl wouldn't do what

Mayor O'Roon wanted. He said Mart Goebel was glad enough to do it. Mart is bigger than Karl. They say he's even stronger. But he's slower. Karl can lick him, any day. Just the same, everyone's afraid of Mart. Especially on payday evening, when he has a few drinks in him. He's always hard up, too. And he won't mind swearing to such a lie as the mayor is coaching him in. Before the chief and the deputies can stop the fight, he's liable to pretty near kill you, Mr. Blayne," she quavered. "That's why I sneaked around here. To beg you not to go home through Durkin Lane, tonight — or any night — and to —"

"I'm thanking you. I'm thanking you good and plenty, Miss," Denny assured her. "Gee, but it'd be turrible if a poor little helpless cuss, like me, was to be beat up by a gre't monster like this Mart Goebel bruiser! Thanks for — for — WAIT!!!" he roared, his face suddenly alight.

He cast aside his mock terror and fairly danced up and down; on the strength of one of his marvelous inspirations.

Hildreth and Greta eyed him with bewilderment. But before either of them could speak, he mumbled, drunkenly rapturous:

"Your dad has an A-1 good name in this town, so I hear. His word in court would be worth more'n the average. Brant tells me your uncle is a priest, too. Your priest uncle wrote me a real beautiful letter about the trifling wee

133

peckle I was able to do to help you out. I'm going round to see him. I'm going to see your dad, too. They can cash in on some of that extry gratitood of theirs, if they're a mind to. Then I'll chase over to the State Police barracks and sing a little song to Sergeant Crayne. Crayne's square. And he likes a good fight and he likes a good joke; and he hates that Coult outfit like toadpie. Oh, it's a wow! Come along, the two of you. Come, *quick!*"

Peaceful late afternoon had settled on the town of Sark. Shadows were beginning to draw toward the sunset. Soft summer light bathed the houses and roads. It was the supper hour; a time when nine tenths of Sark's population were in their own homes.

From the *Bugle* office emerged Brant Hildreth and Denny Blayne; on their way to their evening meal at Brant's mother's.

Like most other printers, Denny was scrupulously neat and spruce in his personal appearance, outside of his work place and work hours. But this afternoon he wore shabby trousers and a pair of split old sneaker-shoes and a torn black sweater, and no hat.

The partners strolled, chatting gaily, down the street, to the entrance of Durkin Lane, a narrow and unpaved back byway, leading through vacant lots and fields toward the Hildreth homestead a half-mile distant. The lane lay empty and lonely, between its occasional patches of copse and undergrowth.

The two men reached and crossed the bridge from which, a few nights earlier, Denny had vaulted into the pond hole in pursuit of Greta Melvin. They were walking in leisurely fashion. Denny seemed unwontedly gay.

Twenty yards beyond the bridge a figure entered the lane from behind an intersecting hedge line, and came toward them. It was a man, huge and heavy-set and ill-clad. He walked with a roll which seemed rather overdone, and he was scowling savagely at the world at large.

Brant stopped and knelt down to tie a loosened shoelace. Denny walked slowly onward. The large and scowling man came almost abreast of him. Politely, even cringingly, Denny Blayne stepped to one side of the narrow lane to give him full room to pass. But the big man would not have it so. He thrust out an unwashed hand and gave Denny a shove, to clear the way still further. Again, meekly, Denny gave ground, wordless and humble. Mart Goebel followed him up, striking him across the mouth with the flat of his left hand.

"I didn't touch you! And I didn't speak to you!" announced Denny at the top of his lungs, still making no move to resent the shove and the ensuing slap. "I don't know you, and I never did you any harm. I ask you please to let me alone."

He shrilled the pacific speech as though he had been at some pains to learn it by heart.

135

Mart Goebel's reply was a cuff over the ear that sent Blayne reeling.

Then, with startling suddenness several things began to occur.

Brant Hildreth had finished tying his shoe. He arose to his feet again. With no more than mild impersonal interest, he beheld the unprovoked assault upon his undersized partner. But he did not rush to the ill-treated little man's rescue.

Instead, Hildreth seated himself deliberately upon a rock, some fifteen feet away from Mart Goebel and the bullied Denny Blayne. There, crossing his legs, Brant drew forth his pipe and filled and lighted it. The most prejudiced onlooker could not possibly have accused him of the remotest part in what was taking place five yards away from him.

Mart Goebel's open-handed blow landed full and resoundingly on the side of Denny's head; causing Blayne to stagger. Mart lurched toward him, swearing foully; bent on following up the punishment.

In a trice the meekly timid little Blayne was transformed into a whirlwind fighting machine.

Chapter XVI

Goebel saw vaguely the black-sweatered victim whirl about and charge with head down. Mart's swaggeringly insolent blow whizzed harmless over the flash-swift Denny's head. In the same instant, Goebel was aware of a series of snappingly thudding rapid-fire fist punches that tore into his over-plump stomach and tattooed against his heart.

There is a mile of difference between the best amateur rough-and-tumble fighter and a professional pugilist. For one thing, the latter has ever a snap and a sting and a crushing power to his punch which almost no amateur acquires and which the sluggishly slow Mart Goebel had never learned nor hitherto experienced.

The fearsome short-arm close-quarters blows smashed against Goebel's wind and heart with sickening force. They shook and nauseated and tortured their dazed recipient. As he strove to grapple with Blayne, the latter danced nimbly back out of reach, on the way landing an uppercut with cruel stinging power against the Adam's apple of Goebel's thick throat.

Before Mart could set himself, Blayne had bored in again; a crushing left-hander to the wind making the big fellow crouch instinctively forward, the breath clean knocked out of him.

To crouch forward, one must lower the chin. Mart Goebel's fleshy jaw was duly lowered by his convulsive doubling over.

In the tiniest fraction of a second, Denny set himself. With all his skill and trained strength and snappiness, he drove his bare right fist to a spot perhaps half an inch to the left of the point of Mart Goebel's down-moving chin.

The impact of the scientifically hammered punch sounded like the crack of a pistol. The beefy knees of Mart Goebel melted like hot tallow. The beefy body of Mart Goebel slumped at the middle like a shot squirrel's. To the ground he tumbled, face forward, oblivious, for the time, of all the mundane happenings of this world of strife.

A knocked-down man usually falls on his back. A completely knocked-*out* fighter almost always collapses, face downward. Mart Goebel fell prone on his face, his body spread-eagled. He quivered all over; then lay very still.

The fight had lasted for less than a handful of seconds. Yet it had left Goebel with a fractured jaw and a ruptured stomach and one cracked rib. Assuredly, Denny Blayne had not studied in vain the punitive tactics of the East-side toughs whence he had sprung. His three years in the prize ring had borne rich fruit, this day, against a clumsy rough-and-tumbler of almost twice his weight and a head taller than he.

The fight was over — over before it seemed to be fairly under way.

Brant Hildreth continued to sit placidly on the rock, puffing away at his pipe and surveying the two combatants with serene unconcern. It was as though he were looking on at a play in which he could have no possible role except that of casual spectator.

Denny glanced at his prostrate and huddled foe and then at the barked knuckles of his right hand. He paid no heed at all to Brant. Nor did his twinkling little eyes so much as wander in the direction of his philosophically smoking partner.

Three men debouched around the end of the hedge, from behind which Goebel had made his entrance on the dramatically brief scene of his fight. The three were Cady, young police chief of Sark, and two of Coult's deputy sheriffs. They bore down upon Denny.

Their approach was truculent. But it was easy to see they were all three rattled and nonplused by the wholly unforeseen phase the encounter had taken. However, the chief seemed bent on acting out his own assigned part in the performance. Laying a hand on Denny's shoulder, he declaimed:

"Dennis Blayne, you're my prisoner. On charges of felonious assault with intent to kill; and of disorderly conduct in forcing a fight on this poor inoffensive feller you've committed the said assault and battery and mayhem upon. And —"

"Ain't you getting some of your law terms kind of pied, Mr. Chief?" asked Denny. "I thought the —"

"Also, Brant Hildreth," continued Chief Cady, facing the moveless Brant, "I arrest you as accessory and accomplice to Blayne in this homicidal attack on Martin Goebel. You and Blayne assaulted him, one from each side, as Goebel was walking peaceably about his business. I witnessed the entire assault, as I happened to be coming along this lane. These two sworn deputy sheriffs were with me and they can testify to what I saw. They —"

"Chief," spoke up Hildreth, "do you actually mean to tell us, as an officer of the law, that the version you've just given of the affair is true? Are you prepared to swear to it in open court?"

"Yes. And I warn you both that anything you say is liable to be used against you. Will you come along quiet, or — ?"

He blinked over Hildreth's shoulder toward a bramble-laced sumac copse, some ten yards distant. From its hollowed center several people were emerging. The foremost of them was in clerical garb. Behind him came Sergeant Crayne, of the New Jersey State Police. Behind Crayne walked Greta Melvin's father. Greta's husky brother, Karl, was the last of the group.

Quietly they advanced toward the men surrounding the senseless Goebel, as one of the deputies knelt to apply first aid to the knocked-out tough. It was Sergeant Crayne who spoke.

"Good evening, Chief," said he. "These gentlemen and I happened to be sitting in that copse, yonder, just by accident, chatting about twenty minutes ago, when we saw you come along with those deputies of yours and with Mart Goebel. You all four went behind that hedge. Then one of the deputies came out and went to the corner down yonder where the lane runs into Sussex Street. A few minutes later he came running back, and we heard him yell to you: 'They've started this way.' It didn't make any sense to us, of course, but we got kind of curious. So we just stayed where we were; and we used our eyes and our ears."

Chief Cady's mouth fell ajar. Then it snapped shut, and he made as though to speak. But the sergeant went on, unheeding:

"We saw Goebel come out from where you were hiding. We saw him hit Mr. Blayne twice, and we heard him swear at him, too. We can take oath Mr. Blayne moved out of the man's way without hitting back, and that all Mr. Blayne said was to beg Goebel not to hit him. It wasn't till Goebel swatted him the third time that Blayne even tried to defend himself. As for Mr. Hildreth, he wasn't in on any of it. That's the truth, and you know well it's the truth. Likewise, we can swear we just heard you try to frame these two men. We can swear to the story you said you were going to tell in court. Gentlemen," turning to his three companions, "have I given the right version of this, or haven't I?"

The three nodded emphatic assent.

"Now, then," summed up the sergeant, "go ahead with your frame-up arrest, Chief. Take these two prisoners of yours to court, to-morrow morning. And you and these deputies swear to your story. I'll be there, to swear to what I saw and heard. So will my friends here. Perhaps the oaths of a reverend priest of the Church and of a state troopers' sergeant and of two highly respected Sark citizens, like the Melvins, will outweigh your handmade yarn. Even Coult's pet judge, Bogardus, won't have the nerve to take your testimony against ours, and you know it. If he does, we'll get a change of venue and carry the case higher. Along with an affidavit from Mr. Karl Melvin that this whole thing was staged, and that he was offered a hundred dollars to take Goebel's job in it. Then there'll be a new police chief in Sark. And maybe a man named Cady in jail for per-jury. And two deputies with him. How about it?"

Before the flabbergasted chief could reply, one of the deputies announced loudly:

"That's good, with me. I didn't see anything and I didn't hear anything. I'm out!"

He spun on his heel and made off, townward, along the sunset lane. The second deputy ceased from his Samaritan labors over the slowly recovering Mart Goebel, and incontinently took to his heels in the wake of his departing companion.

"Your two witnesses seem all wet, Chief," commented the sergeant. "It seems there'll just be your own unsupported word, against all of our evidence. I doubt if Coult will be lunkhead enough to let the charge be pressed, with that much weight against him."

"Maybe — maybe I spoke a bit quick and thoughtless," stammered the young chief. "I was so excited by the fight that most likely I got things a little twisted. The best of us will do that, sometimes, and —"

"The *best* of us?" repeated Denny, innocently. "How do *you* know?"

Chief Cady eyed him, right balefully; but chose wisely to ignore the slur.

"The arrest don't go," said he. "I couldn't see and hear what went on, so very good, from 'way back where I was. Maybe I was mistaken. I'll just take your word on it, Sergeant, and let it drop."

He was about to move off in the same direction as his recreant accomplices had gone, when Denny Blayne halted him.

"Do I understand there's no charge against me?" he asked.

"Didn't I just tell you so?" snapped the chief, peevishly, as he moved on.

"Wait!" commanded Denny. "Come back here! There's going to be a charge made to *you*, right here and now, as chief of police of this township. I'm going to make it, and I'm going to back it on the testimony of all these gentlemen who saw what went on."

He pointed with one thumb at Mart Goebel. Mart was sitting up and blinking owlishly about him; both hands nursing his broken jaw, as he moaned lamentably and spat forth blood.

"Chief," continued Denny, "I charge this man with — with — Aw, what's the words, Brant?" he demanded. "I can't remember everything in the world, can I?"

"With malicious and unprovoked assault," prompted Hildreth, "and disorderly conduct."

"Likewise and also," added Denny, smitten by the thought of a desirable addition to the formal accusations, "likewise and also I charge him with committing willful mayhem on me by lac'rating and abrading and contoosing the knuckles of my right hand with that scrap-iron jaw of his. Orf'cer, do your dooty! These gents will all appear in court as my witnesses, tomorrer, when I press the charge. Run him in, Chief. We're looking at you."

With a visage of utter sourness, Cady glared at the group. Then, as if glad to find someone on whom to vent his impotent wrath and humiliation, he gripped the slowly rising and still stupefied Mart Goebel by the shirt collar and hauled him to his feet; propelling the beaten tough in front of him as he went toward the town.

"We'll all just ramble along with you," suggested Denny, "to keep you comp'ny and to see your pris'ner don't break away before you get him to the coop. I'm on my way there, anyhow, to make the formal charge against him, at the desk, so there won't be any blunder in entering it on the blotter. Them blunders has happened, sometimes, you know."

Aschar Coult sat well back from the window in his private office, in the Sark courthouse. With him sat Ralph Cormick and Mayor O'Roon and one or two other local officials. Unseen from outside, they commanded a full view of the square end of the street-mouths opening into it.

For some minutes they had sat thus, expectantly, talking little and eying the square with watchful anticipation. From either one of the two street-ends they expected momentarily to see Chief Cady emerge into the square, reinforced by Coult's two stalwart deputies; the three conveying Brant Hildreth and Denny Blayne, duly handcuffed and hauled along as by needful force. It was a sweet anticipation to all the clump of spectators.

"I see them!" suddenly announced Cormick. "There! Coming out of Sussex Street. They —"

His mouth went slack. Wordless, aghast, the watchers stared.

Out into the square strode Chief Cady, distorted of face, hangdog, infuriated. He was pushing along by the collar a man, evidently much hurt, whose face was a mask of drying blood, and who could barely keep upon his stumbling feet.

A single tense look told Coult and the other spectators that this prisoner was not either of the *Bugle*'s owners; but that unquestionably he was their doughty paladin, Mart Goebel.

Behind the chief and his badly mauled prisoner walked in merry converse Brant Hildreth and Denny Blayne; in company with Sergeant Crayne and the priest and the two Melvins. Behind and around them clustered a fast-increasing crowd of townsfolk. To each and all of these, Denny was recounting the saga of Goebel's downfall and of the criminal charge the chief had tried to fasten upon the victor and on Brant.

Chapter XVII

The power and majesty of the law, as typified by Preakness County, could not be exercised against Mart Goebel. Unfortunately for justice, the desperate prisoner managed to escape from his cell in the jail wing of the courthouse, sometime during the night. Presumably, he got away clean to the Ramapo Mountains where there were a hundred inaccessible hiding places and where "Jackson White" friends and kinsmen of his could be relied upon to shelter him.

All this, though the doctor who attended Mart in his cell, an hour before his escape, found the prisoner too badly injured to be moved to the county hospital until an ambulance could be brought for him in the morning. In brief, the crushed and half-dead Goebel had been spirited away during the night by those who had access to his locked cell. Thus, the case must perforce be dropped, for lack of a defendant.

All of which Brant Hildreth pointed out in the next issue of the *Bugle*; along with Karl Melvin's affidavit of the part he had been asked to take in the transaction. The Mart Goebel case was the leading feature of this next issue's front page.

Openly, the *Bugle* accused Chief Cady of malfeasance; and of attempted perjury, to deprive two innocent men of their liberty. By almost an open implication, Brant's leading editorial accused Sheriff Aschar Coult of planning this ruse; in order to silence the *Bugle* by imprisoning its editors.

There was much, in that issue, about the high school secret societies and of the steps already afoot to abolish them. But, next to the Goebel story, the leading feature of the paper was a detailed account, by "Old Roman" of the way the local liquor traffic was run, in defiance of the law; and of the transporting of illicit liquor through the county by the connivance of and at the profit of the county's own sheriff.

Condensed, the situation it outlined was much like that which was proven to be in vogue in a hundred rural regions from the Atlantic to the Pacific and from Maine to Florida; during the prohibition and post-prohibition years.

To eastward, a ragged ribbon of Preakness County extended almost to the Hudson River. To southward it ran to New Jersey's more central counties. Coastwise steamships of light draught and sloops, plying from Jacksonville to Maryland, ostensibly for fruit and vegetable cargoes, would run into New York harbor, make their declarations; and thence would go up the Hudson to deliver their perishable freight to wholesale consignees in Newburgh,

Peekskill, Poughkeepsie and lesser towns.

Beneath the vegetable and fruit crates, on some of them, were hidden cases of liquor, picked up clandestinely at their various ports of call along the coast. By night, great and rapid trucks would roll to the private docks where the boats were tied up, and would take away loads of this illicit cargo.

As there were Federal agents, everywhere, on the lookout for such lawless traffic, it behooved the trucks to find some route whereby they could best proceed uninterrupted to their destinations. Therefore, the promoters of the scheme sought roads through counties whose officials could be made to keep their eyes and ears shut, in return for heavy bribes. Such highways are technically known to the bootleg fraternity as "greased roads." Such a county, according to "Old Roman," was Preakness.

The letter went on to tell the wages paid to the daring drivers of these trucks — averaging from $1.75 to $2.25 per mile, according to the comparative safety or danger of the route — and the "retaining fee" paid to garages along the roads for furnishing shelter to the trucks for "staches" (overnight rests) and for answering on the jump any code telephone call from the drivers at any hour in the twenty-four. For harboring or tending these trucks the garage men's fee ranged from $20 to $35 per night or per day. Hurry-up jobs were paid for at proportionately high rates.

Incidentally, said "Old Roman," many under-salaried peace justices and police chiefs and constables, along the greased roads, had been buying costly radios and new cars; or were re-furnishing their homes in extravagant fashion or installing player pianos and other luxuries. All this by virtue of unexplainedly sudden wealth from some mysterious source.

"Old Roman" not only gave a categorical schedule of the tariffs, but named nine or ten petty Preakness County officials, (citing their known salaries) who had bought of late several grossly expensive possessions, wholly out of keeping with their pay. He left his readers to form their own conclusions. He did not in so many words accuse these men of accepting bribes from the bootleg interests.

But, boldly and without reservations, he de-clared that Aschar Coult was shielding and helping the malefactors and was profiting thereby. He said that if necessary he would bring forward proofs to back this claim.

He said more: He told of the illicit ("moon-shine") stills conducted by the so-called "Jackson Whites" — an illiterate and degen-erate set of hillbillies who lived in the Ramapo Mountains at the inner edge of the county. He said they were known to be devoted to Coult; who not only had guarded them from Federal suspicion but who was a silent partner in their enterprises, enabling them to dispose of their products without molestation.

The letter was a terrific arraignment. With

his eyes open, Brant Hildreth printed it, verbatim. This by reason of a strange intuitive faith he had grown to feel in the nameless writer. Not once, hitherto, had Coult denied "Old Roman's" most vitriolic accusations, nor taken overt notice of them; even though he must have realized that every line in every letter was undermining the courthouse gang's power and was rousing an increasingly strong public feeling against the grafters.

Brant reasoned that, were not the charges true and were not Coult fearful lest they be substantiated on request, he would have taken legal measures, before now, to punish them. Coult assuredly must feel that the *Bugle* would not have the breathtaking audacity to print them, if it did not have full proof to back its libel-tempting assertions. The anonymity of the writer was in itself a safeguard against action by Coult.

"Old Roman's" charges, Aschar evidently feared, were written by a resentful member of his own ring — a member who, undoubtedly, had furnished Brant with proofs of his accusations. Without such proof, the most reckless editor was not likely to have taken chances on legal punishment by printing the denunciatory screeds.

It was on this putative belief of Coult's which Hildreth relied for safety. And, week by week, he was more and more certain that his own supposition as to the sheriffs non-resentment was correct. For Coult had given no sign.

Altogether, this latest issue of the *Bugle* was more bombshell-like in its contents than had been any of its predecessors. From the hour of its appearance on the street, the town had been in a state of buzzing excitement. On his way to and from the office that day — and on leaving church the next morning — and by telephone calls and telegrams — Hildreth was apprised of the growing endorsement of the large decent element of the community.

Denny shone as a public hero. The fact that he could thrash a bully of almost double his weight — the news that once he had actually been a professional prize fighter — all this, atop of his rescue of Greta Melvin from the pond hole — came close to turning the smugly delighted little East-sider into a local idol. Yet there was a fly in the ointment of Denny's grinning contentment at his new exaltation.

"All these handshakers and back-swatters who stop me on the street," he complained as he and Hildreth were beginning work at the office on Monday morning, "well, of course, it's all right, so far as it goes. But what is it they glad-hand me about? It's that dead-easy licking I gave Goebel, and the muddying I got when I fished the Melvin kid out'n that measly pond hole. Not a word, mind you, about my 'Seen in Sark' column. That's the best noospaper stuff that ever hit this smalltime burg. But not a word do folks say about it. If they've got to hold me up every few steps to backswat me and pumphandle me, why can't they do it for the real worth-while thing I do, and not just for them two bushleague stunts of mine? At that," he finished, philosophically, "I got no kick coming. We seem to have Friend Coult beat to a standstill, in spite of all them croakings of yours about his being stronger than what I thought. This last *Bugle* has sure put him down for the count."

"Or else waked him up to come back at us," pessimistically suggested Brant, obsessed by a growing worry he could not define and which had been growing more and more acute for the past few hours. "Our latest punch, as you may call it, may only be a Pyrrhic victory for us."

"Pyrrhic?" repeated Denny, puzzled. "Who's Pyrrhic? I never heard of him. Must have done his winning on one of the western tracks. Anyhow — Say, at Church, yesterday, that priest of mine, spoke about a fight, in the old times — most likely before George Washington was born. A scrap between a lad named David and a heavyweight named Goliath. I didn't rightly get the hang of the whole story. But it seems this David was put up against the heavyweight champion, for a finish battle. And David wasn't anything but a kid. He must have been a featherweight, at that; from all I could understand. I'm going to ask the priest, some time, how that fight came out. But what I want to know, most, is what David's manager was

153

thinking about, to match his man against the Big Feller. He was cuckoo; that manager was. Or else maybe he was crooked. A fight like that wouldn't draw a rainy-night house in the backwoods. It —"

The whirr of the telephone interrupted him. Brant took up the instrument. For perhaps a minute, he listened intently, his face grim. Then, after a word or two in acknowledgment, he hung up the receiver and faced Denny.

Chapter XVIII

"I think you said Aschar Coult was beaten," said Hildreth, dully. "Well, he isn't. That call was from Crayne. He's pretty hot under the collar. Old Melvin has just phoned him to ask the troopers' help in finding Karl."

"Karl?" echoed Denny. "Oh, you mean his son, Karl Melvin."

"Who in blazes else would I mean?" snapped Hildreth, his frayed nerves twitching at the inane question.

"Well, don't get woozy over it," counseled Denny. "First off, when you said 'Karl,' I was thinking of Karl Pieters, up the street. The funny cuss with the home-brewed face; who asked me to learn him to box. He — What about Karl Melvin, anyhow?" he broke off his vapid explanation. "Why does his dad want the troopers to help find him? The boy is too big to get lost in any common-sized room, ain't he? And if he went outdoors, he can likely find his own way back. What's all the excitement about?"

"The excitement," answered Brant, his voice heavy with worry, "the excitement is — late last night, Karl got a phone call, just as he was going to bed. The call was supposed to be from a road-house owner up on the Newton road, who said Karl's chum, Phil Damer, had just been carried into his inn, smashed and dying from an automobile collision. And that Phil wanted to give Karl a last message for his girl, who's away at Newark, on a visit. Karl went off in a rush, on his bicycle. He has never come back."

"Huh?" grunted Denny, newly interested. "Decoy stuff, hey? His dad goes to the road-house or phones to it, and he finds no such message was ever sent from there? He — ?"

"He went. He didn't phone. The proprietor said he hadn't sent the message and that nobody was brought to his house from any accident. It's a lonely road, especially that time of night. On the way back, just where a wood-lane joins the road, Melvin found Karl's bicycle, crumpled up in a ditch. There were a lot of stamping and shuffling footmarks all around it, and some splashes of blood on the grass and leaves. Karl must have put up a good fight, before someone slugged him from behind and put him out of commission. That's all Melvin knows. So he called up the troopers and —"

"And our dear old buddy, Chief Cady, and Sheriff Coult," suggested Denny, "and —"

"No," denied Brant. 'No, he didn't. Crayne says Melvin told him he knew it wouldn't be any use."

"*Why* wouldn't it be any use?" argued Denny.

"What's the Sark police and the sheriff for, if it ain't to hunt down crooks that don't pay for protection? And a bunch of rube hold-up men wouldn't be likely to make enough, per month, in this hick neighborhood, to pay protection money to the police or the sheriff. Fact is, I can't see why they took all that bother to hold up a working chap like Karl Melvin. Karl couldn't have had more'n a few dollars on him, at most. So —"

"If they had been thieves, they would have stolen his bicycle, too," said Hildreth. "They might have knocked him over the head when he resisted. But they'd have gone through his clothes for cash and for his watch and any other things worth stealing. And then they'd have left him there. Why should thieves carry away a senseless man, after they'd robbed him?"

"Unless they'd hit too hard by mistake, and croaked him," pondered Denny; adding impatiently: "But, no; that's another fool crack of mine. If they'd killed him, they'd have left him laying where he was and they'd have cleared out, on the jump. Unless — unless they'd bother to stick him into the woods, so's he mightn't be found so quick. But even that would be a crazy thing to do. They'd either leave him lay, or else they'd drag him out into the road, so folks would think a car had hit him. Nope, it wasn't hold-ups that got the poor cuss."

"No," agreed Brant, "it wasn't."

Hildreth's face was set and gloomy. To cheer

him, Blayne continued with sprightly optimism:

"Well, anyhow, he wasn't any twin brother of ours. And besides, it'll write up, grand, in this week's *Bugle*. It —"

"This week's *Bugle*," interposed Brant, speaking with slow despondency, "probably won't be brought out."

"Why the Sam Hill won't it be brought out?" challenged Denny. "We've got paper enough and we've got cash enough and we've got ads and news enough. If I and you don't drop dead —"

"Or drop into two cells at the courthouse," corrected Hildreth, "under heavier bail than we can pay. Denny, don't you see, even yet, what this thing means?"

"No," said Blayne, sulkily, "I don't. So s'pose you stop looking like the First C'nspir'tor, and take time off to tell me. What's the big idee, anyhow?"

Mrs. Hildreth's surly old man-of-all-work slouched homeward past the office window, from an errand in the town. Brant knocked on the pane and beckoned him in.

"Take Thane home with you," he ordered, slipping a leash on the dog's collar. "Ask my mother to keep him tied up and to take care of him. Tell her Mr. Blayne and I may not be at home again for a day or two. Tell her it's all right, and she isn't to worry. Trot along, Thane."

As the man departed, convoying the reluctant collie, Hildreth turned back to Denny who sat writhing with inquisitive eagerness.

"You want to know the main idea?" said Brant. "Well, here it is, in just a few words."

"Let's have them same few words. Spill 'em fast."

"In the first place, Coult and his gang have been after us, ever since they found they or we would have to clear out of the county. First they tried to buy us off, and then to scare us off and then to frame us. They lost out, on all three —"

"Yep. That's ancient history. Keep moving! What — ?"

"Unless they wanted to kill us — and that would be too risky, even for them — the quickest and easiest way to abolish us and our paper would be to jail us on some charge, and have one of their judges put the bail too high for us to pay. We could be kept locked up for months, before our trial, that way. A packed jury could find us guilty, then, and send us to the cells for a year or so longer. We'd be bottled. And the *Bugle* would be dead. The paper's crusades would only be remembered as the efforts of a pair of jailbirds to muckrake a peaceful community. Besides —"

"So you've been saying," yawned Denny. "But I still don't get the wild excitement. And I don't see what Karl Melvin has to do with —"

"Shut up! " adjured Hildreth. "I'm coming to

that, soon enough. I wanted to make the rest of it plain to you, so you'd catch my drift when I get to the point."

"Sorry," muttered Blayne. "Shoot. I'll stay muzzled."

"They lost out when they tried to frame us on that assault and battery charge, and on the charge of carrying deadly weapons," went on Brant. "But those were piker charges compared with criminal libel. If they can get us on criminal libel for anything, the public can be made to think we've been libeling them in everything we've said. That kills our work here."

"Sure. But —"

"There is a ton of dynamite in every one of 'Old Roman's' letters. But Coult is afraid to bring suit against us for those. He's afraid we're standing in with whoever writes them; and that he's given us his proofs. That muzzles Coult. That's why he's been so wild to find out which one of his crowd is betraying him."

"We've been just as wild to find out who it is, as Coult is. He —"

"But at last he's found something he *can* get us on; and get us good and plenty, at that. The last *Bugle* ran Karl Melvin's affidavit that Coult and O'Roon tried to hire him to beat us up. Then I wrote a news story, and an editorial, besides, telling the same thing and saying it was a conspiracy on the part of sworn officers of the law to send two innocent men to prison. I was safe in saying that. For Karl was willing to testify in court to the truth of what I said. Without Karl to back me, my story and editorial are basis for a criminal libel suit. Coult or O'Roon or Cady could sue us, personally. Or the county itself could sue; as I understand it. Anyhow, there is a big criminal libel case against us, as owners of the paper that printed the stuff.

"So what does the gang do? They lure Karl Melvin — our only possible witness — out into a lonely place; and they slug him into unconsciousness and carry him away somewhere. Perhaps up into one of the Ramapo Mountain caves, with a bunch of armed Jackson White moonshiners to keep him safe. Perhaps they shanghaied him aboard one of the bootleg sloops over on the Hudson. Wherever they've put him, they'll see he stays out of the way for a good long time. Perhaps forever.

"That gives them a clear case against us. It means we may both be under arrest any minute now, for criminal libel. Criminal libel means jail. Not just a fine. Coult will see the bail is prohibitive. Denny, they've got us. Nobody around here has enough interest in us, or enough pluck, to antagonize the gang by going our bail. Nobody except my mother. And she hasn't enough money or property to meet such bail as Emerson Bogardus will set."

Denny had listened to much of the speech with vibrant emotion. But, for the last minute, he had grown philosophically calm, with the true stoicism of his class. Now, he arose and stretched himself.

"Well," he remarked, with casual phlegm, "if I gotta stay in the coop, I'm due to get one of my bum headaches. And it's a cinch Coult won't have someone chase out and get me any headache powders. So, I'll just toddle over to the drugstore and lay me in a few. Back in a few minutes. Bye-bye."

Frowningly, Hildreth watched the callous little man saunter across the street to the druggist's, and vanish within the store. Brant was disgusted with his partner's dearth of sympathy and of concern in their impending fate. He could not understand this new phase in the excitable Blayne's character.

But he had no time for disapproval or for conjecture. The office door swung wide, and Aschar Coult strolled in, wooden-faced and imperturbable as ever.

"You've come to serve the warrant yourself, eh?" Brant greeted him. "That's a genuine honor. We were waiting for the arrest. But we didn't dare hope the sheriff himself would do the job. You're certainly democratic and neighborly, Coult."

"You're a grand good guesser, Boy," drawled Coult, approvingly. "I figured you'd have heard about Karl Melvin's sneaking out of the jurisdiction of our court, by this time; and that you'd know what it would mean to you. You've guessed it right. Want me to serve the warrant formally and tap you on the shoulder and say the words and warn you about your rights and all the rest of that rigmarole? Or will you and Blayne come along to the courthouse with me, quiet and nice? Either way suits *me*."

Through the window, Brant could see several deputies and two local patrolmen loitering on the sidewalk. Through the window, too, he could see Denny Blayne crossing the street from the drugstore, his cherished headache powders clutched in his hand.

"We'll come along quietly," answered Qildreth. "Here's Blayne, now. Just wait till I lock my desk and shut up the rest of the place. It may be some little time before we get back here, you know."

"If *I* don't know it, Boy," said Coult, happily, "then nobody does. But your ideas of 'some little time' are apt to be several hundred times too conservative. By the time you and your friend are at large again, there won't be any more *Bugle*. So, say good-by to it. You've had a real nice time here. But it had to end. And it's ending, for keeps."

"Coult," observed Denny, airily, as he and Brant fell into step on either side of the sheriff, the deputies bringing up the rear, "just by looking at you, I can tell your mother must have been turrible fond of children. She'd never have bothered to raise *you*, if she wasn't."

Chapter XIX

Brant Hildreth sat drearily on the edge of his hard wall bunk in the first of a basement tier of nine cells which constituted the "lock-up" of the Preakness County courthouse's jail wing. For nearly seven hours he had sat thus, miserable, the future stretching forth before him as stark and barren as a rainy sea.

There he had sat alone and untended throughout the lush summer's day. Ever since he had been led thither by a turnkey after his few minutes' presence in the magistrate's smelly little court, abovestairs, to which Sheriff Aschar Coult had led him and Denny Blayne on their arrival at the courthouse.

In the upstairs room, beneath a fresco of Blind Justice, County Judge Emerson Bogardus had listened while a clerk rattled off the indictment against them. The judge was a youngish and swarthy man, oily of skin and with outjuts of jet-black hair and beard and with many virulent pimples. Brant remembered him in boyhood as that most atrocious of pests, the village cut-up. Now, in his early thirties, he presided as county judge, at the behest of Aschar Coult whose adoringly obedient tool and henchman he was proud to be.

Having heard the hasty preliminaries, Judge Emerson Bogardus had held the two defendants in twenty-five thousand dollars' bail each, to answer at the October assizes to a charge of criminal libel, *in re* the article and the editorial printed in the *Bugle*, two days earlier, concerning an alleged attempt to bribe one Karl Melvin to conspire against the due course of justice.

Failing to produce the requisite bail, the two were taken thence to the tier of cells in the jail-wing basement. There, for the past seven hours had Brant Hildreth sat, alone and brooding.

He was brooding over the arrant failure of his efforts to cleanse and build up the county his father had loved and worked for, and to deliver it from the looters who sucked dry its sustenance and exploited it for greed.

He had made a good fight — with the eager help of Denny Blayne — to cut this mammoth plague spot from his home county, and to restore it to its ancient glories. He had hoped his work was beginning to bear fruit — to awaken the decent people of the county to their own wrongs — to rouse them to their own best interests. And now —

From the adjoining cell arose, raucous and jocund, the voice of Denny Blayne. At intervals throughout the long day Denny had striven to lighten his own servitude and that of the tier's other inmates by occasional remarks which

165

ranged all the way from cheery to ribald. Once or twice he had even lifted his voice in song; to the condemning horror of such officials and attendants as the strident tones chanced to reach. Now he declaimed, piercingly:

"Nothing's so black as what it seems. When things is at their blackest, just take a good squint at Aschar Coult. And you'll see he's a lot blacker. And slimier. Likewise lousier. Besides, he's —"

An attendant, dispatched by the warden, bade him be silent. To the scandalized messenger Denny's voice rose afresh, in piteous appeal:

"Can't you borrow a can opener, son, and let me have it? If it's a halfway up-to-date can opener, I can pry my way out of this comic opera junk shop in eight seconds. I could do it with a hairpin if I hadn't left mine on the grand piano, at home. Of all the jails I ever was in, this is the punkest. Tell Coult's henchman, Judge Bogardus, from me — tell him: 'Henchperson, Mister Blayne says —'"

"Silence, there, you!" commanded the attendant, majestically. "Shut up, or it'll be the worse for you."

"How'll it be the worse for me?" insisted Denny. "They can't put me any further into the coop than they did, can they? Say, Drizzle-Puss, while I think of it, tell that cross-eyed warden of yours that the champagne at lunch was too warm and the burgundy wasn't warm enough. And he can't persuade me that that caviar was beluga. It was cheap domestic stuff. So was the camembert. I won't stand for such privations. The lobster thermidor was —"

"You'll stop that noise, or —"

"And if you see my old college chummy, Aschar Coult, tell him one of these days I'm going to duck him headfirst into a water bucket. I'm going to duck his head into it three times; and I ain't going to pull his head out of it but twice. Now, trot along, sonny, and fetch me my Rolls-Royce. I left it on the corner of the courtroom desk."

Loftily, the attendant stalked away, bitterly regretting that the primitive jail was not equipped with a dark cell or a dungeon, wherein the impudent captive might be thrust.

As he departed, Blayne burst into shrill song; his ditty carrying easily to the floors above and even to the square beyond. The tune was "Botany Bay." The words were an inspired paraphrase of that classic Limehouse lyric's second verse:

*"Seven long weary hours have I been here
And Lord knows how long I must stay,
Just for proving Asch Coult a cheap grafter
And giving his gyp tricks away."*

The singer fell silent, while he groped for a new impromptu verse. For a few moments, stillness sagged over the row of cells. Then

167

down the damp corridor clumped the heavy tread of the attendant, light and fast footsteps close behind him.

"Lady to see you," announced the attendant, unlocking and opening Brant Hildreth's cell.

He stood back, alertly on guard, at the side of the narrow stone hallway. Then, as the dazed Brant got to his feet, Kay Cormick came hurrying into the grim little cubbyhole.

"Kay!" exclaimed Hildreth, incredulous.

He blinked at the bright face and the shimmering white summer dress of the girl. Her presence seemed to glorify the dismal place.

"Kay!"

"I didn't hear of it till half an hour ago," she began, without other greeting than to clasp both his nerveless hands in her own warm little grip. "Nobody seems to have known till then. But somehow it has gotten out, and people are all gathering in the square out yonder. I came here as soon as I heard. I found your bail was twenty-five thousand."

"You shouldn't have come, dear. This is no kind of place for —"

"I own half our house. Ralph owns the other half. Half of it isn't worth that much money. But I've some investments that Mother left me. And I wanted them to take my half of the house and all the investments they'd need for bail. And — and they *won't*. They sent for Ralph. He made an awful scene up there, Brant. He told me to go home. So I came here.

168

The warden knows I'm Ralph's sister, and Ralph got him the position. So he let me come to see you. Ralph wasn't looking. Now, what can I do?"

"Do?" echoed Brant, still dizzy. "*Do?* Why, Kay, your coming here — your caring enough about me to want to help me out — that has been enough. Ten billion times more than enough. I —"

"And won't you please forgive me for being so — so horrible about the school societies? Please, *please* do, Brant! I'm so ashamed! I wanted to write and say so. But — but somehow I couldn't. Won't you be friends again? I CAN'T have you stay in this hideous place. *Tell* me what to do to get you free. I looked everywhere for Aschar Coult. And I telephoned him, too. But he's started off in his car, on one of his official tours of the county. As soon as he gets back — I can't do anything with Ralph —"

"Sorry, Miss," spoke up the fat voice of the fatter warden behind her, "but your brother says I'm to take you away from here, right off. He asked me if I'd seen you, and when he found where you'd gone, he took on something fearful. Please to come along with me, right away, Miss. I'll — I'll have to use force if you don't. He told me to. I — I —"

"Go, Kay," said Brant, softly. "Just this spent minute with you has been worth a lot more to me than you can know. I thank you for it, from the bottom of my heart. Go, please. I don't want you to get into a family squabble on my account. Go. I mean it. You can help me best that way. I'll be all right. Go."

She hesitated, inclining to rebel. Very tenderly, he thrust her from the cell, and clanged shut its door between them. The warden laid a plump and none-too-clean hand on her arm; respectfully but strongly drawing her away. As she went, step by step, the sound of stifled weeping came back to Hildreth. Then —

"For Pete's sake, Brant!" squalled Denny, from the adjoining cell. "Just take a peek out of the winder, onto the square."

Each cell was equipped with a small and foully unwashed window, thickly crossbarred and set high in the wall. At Blayne's sharp exclamation, Hildreth crossed to his own cell's dirty window and scraped some of the grime from a space between two of the bars.

The quaint old square outside was mellow and lovely in the late afternoon sunlight. It was filling fast with folk on foot and in cars and in buggies. The great bulk of the gathering crowd were pedestrians. They were drifting into the square from each ingress, and were grouping and knotting and milling. Slowly the new-formed groups were moving toward the court-house, from every side.

This was no idle throng of curiosity seekers, come to stare at the jail where were incarcerated two scurrilous editors. True, there were a few of the tougher and looser denizens of Sark, strewn through the assemblage. But the vast majority were the solid citizens of town and county; the steady-going element to which the *Bugle* had sought to appeal and whose civic pride it had endeavored to arouse.

The aspect of these men, just now, was grim and coldly determined. There was not a smile to be seen on any of the hundred faces turned toward the jail. Neither was there the look of deviltry nor of foolish ill-temper that marks the average aggressive mob. These men were grim; coldly determined. All of them, except the few local sots and wastrels, had a nameless air of being on sternly important business.

Their eyes held a queer glint of indignation. But their bearing was as controlled as it was resolute. Here was no roaring and irresolutely raging aggregation, but a collection of solid men urged on by a rare common purpose of good citizenship.

Brant Hildreth read aright their expression and the meaning of their presence. Unbidden, a lump came into his throat. A momentary mist hazed his vision. Deep in his heart was born a mighty thankfulness; a sense of life-labor achieved.

What matter, now, if the courthouse gang should be able to hold him and his partner in these cells for months; and then railroad them to prison? The work was done, that he had set out to do. He had been able at last to awaken the decent element of the county to their own danger and to their wrongs at the hands of the looters.

He had kindled a fire which could not be quenched. He was not a failure. Whether or not he should be able to help further in the task, his father's loved county would shake off its graft shackles.

Morbidly, he had told himself that the public read and discussed the *Bugle*, merely as they would grin at a mischievous boy throwing mud at some pompous and unpopular passer-by. He had believed the county was watching his efforts to free it, in the same spirit that it would watch a spectacular street fight. He had not dared to hope that his aim was accomplished; that he had fanned to life the flame of public spirit and of rebellion against dishonest local government.

But the faces of these men in the square told their own story. These were people whose admired and trusted champion was in trouble. They were rallying to his aid.

He had not failed. Coult might wreak what revenge he chose upon the two editors. They had ripped loose the dirty foundations of the gang's political edifice. They had cleared the way for their townsfolk's ultimate freedom and well-being.

An odd sense of exaltation swept Hildreth as he peered out through the dusty little barred pane at the swelling throng. These men meant business, stark and deadly business. They were awake.

Whether or not they would be able to secure the liberty of Denny and himself was a minor matter. The townsfolk would secure their own liberty — the liberty to which the *Bugle* had been urging them so long and so vehemently. The campaign was a success, whatever sour fate might be in store for its two promoters.

A harelipped youth picked up a whitewashed stone; part of the ornamental border of a geranium bed. With baseball-pitcher accuracy, he flung it at the window of Aschar Coult's private office in the courthouse. A muffled tinkle of glass reached Brant's straining ears, to attest the hit.

Instantly, fifty men in the crowd turned on the harelipped youth in hot rebuke. Two of them hustled him bodily from the square. The spirit of this gathering was not the spirit of mischief nor of destructiveness.

A man stepped up on the base of the squat war monument which graced the square's centre. He was Greta Melvin's father; solidly respectable in his best suit of black diagonals and his derby hat. At an imperative gesture of his outstretched arms, the low hum of voices died away. Folk turned to listen. Melvin was a fair representative of the county's sturdily self-respecting workers, the very class Brant had sought to reach and to arouse.

Chapter XX

"Men," came the voice from atop the monument's pedestal, "no use wasting time to explain why we are all here. There wasn't any call sent out for this meeting. But it's a meeting, just the same. A town meeting. Brant Hildreth has been trying for months to break the ring that has been milking our county; the ring that's been making us a disgrace and a laughingstock all over the state. He's opened our eyes to a lot of things we were too lazy or too busy to see by ourselves. He's shown us how to bring back Sark and Preakness County to what they used to be and to what they ought to be now. He's tried to pull us out of the muck that was choking us — just as his partner pulled my little girl out of the muck of the pond hole, down yonder — and to set us on our feet again."

Melvin cleared his heavy voice. Then he went on:

"So now they've jailed him. They've jailed him for printing what my boy told him. My boy that's maybe dead by now because he tried to help Hildreth bust the ring. My boy was the squarest and truthfulest man around here. What he said was true. But they put him where

174

he can't testify to it. And that made them able to arrest Hildreth. Fine gangster trick, hey?"

The rumbling voice had shaken ever so little as Melvin spoke of his kidnaped son. But his words ended in something akin to a snarl. The snarl ran through group after group of his hearers. It was not a pleasant sound, nor reassuring. Melvin continued:

"They're holding him and Blayne in $25,000 bail each, I hear. Now I haven't got $25,000 in the world. Most of us haven't. But I've got part of it. And others of you have got part of it, too. Who'll club in with me to risk enough cash and real estate to make up these two men's bail, and then to start a fund to hire the best lawyers in the state to defend them at their trial? Who'll join up with me in doing that? I —"

He got no further. Instantly the pedestal was surrounded by shouting and arm-waving men; each calling out the amount of money or land he was willing to pledge. Someone drew forth an envelope and a fountain pen, and began to jot down the names and the sums. At once a decorously eager crowd pressed about him, naming the amounts all of them would be responsible for.

As the tally-taker's pen traveled fast over the envelope back, a small procession debouched onto the square, from the courthouse. It was headed by obese Mayor O'Roon. He was followed by Cady, the youthful chief of police; and by Sark's patrolmen. Advancing to the monument, O'Roon signaled loftily for silence. Then, at the top of his lungs, he bawled:

"By the authority vested in me as chief magistrate and mayor of this borough, I command you to disperse and go to your homes. In —"

His pompous pronouncement was drowned in a ripple of laughter from the less solid element of the crowd, and by a low-pitched multiple mutter of dissent from the more respectable majority. Purple with wrath, O'Roon proceeded:

"The police of this borough shall be ordered to clear the square, if you refuse to depart quietly. If they are not strong enough to disperse the rabble, I shall telegraph to the governor for the state militia to quell this riot. *Disperse!*"

His rolling glare fixed itself upon Melvin, standing above him on the pedestal. Melvin made quiet answer:

"This is not a riot. Nor yet it isn't a rabble. It is a representative gathering of peaceful citizens in the public square of their own town. Until you can prove disorder, you have no power to clear the square. A boy smashed a window up there. We disown that act of hoodlumism. I stand ready to pay the damage out of my own pocket. Now," dropping his formal manner, "just you waddle back into your cage, Johnny O'Roon; and take your hand picked cops with you; unless you want us to slap your wrists and then lock you into your own cells along with the two men who would be disgraced by such company. This is a grown men's party — a *white* men's party. There's no room in it for Aschar Coult's dummies nor for bald-headed cheap crooks. Run along, I'm telling you."

A laugh, deep-mouthed, tolerantly amused, from the crowd, greeted the speech. The man with the pen and envelope resumed his interrupted labor of jotting down names and amounts. O'Roon gobbled apoplectically, and turned to give a command to young Cady and the nervous patrolmen.

But the command was not given.

Slowly, through the crowd that made way before it, a dusty limousine, bearing an official license plate, was threading the gravel drive leading across the square to the courthouse. It halted at the foot of the steps. The chauffeur jumped down and held wide the car's door, respectfully helping two very ancient men to descend to the driveway.

The foremost of the two turned to aid the chauffeur in handing the car's other occupant out of the vehicle. Brant Hildreth looked closely at this first man. Then he recognized him as Supreme Court Judge Van Sluyk, whom twice he had interviewed at Trenton, during his own reporter days — one of New Jersey's foremost jurists and publicists, a national figure.

But Brant's attention was shifted instantly from the judge by the advent of the car's other occupant. Tenderly, solicitously, Van Sluyk and the chauffeur were assisting to the ground a long and emaciated and trembling old man, clad in bell-crowned high hat and frock coat.

"Derek Groot!" exclaimed Hildreth, aloud, in utter astonishment. "What in blazes is *he* doing here? That's Van Sluyk's own car, too. It has his initials on it. What in — ?"

He stared, astounded. Mayor O'Roon left his uphill task of dispersing the non-dispersable crowd, and hurried obsequiously forward to welcome the distinguished guest from Trenton. With Van Sluyk and the tottering ex-senator, he passed up the steps and into the courthouse; leaving the turbulent square's management to Cady and the helpless policemen.

A few minutes later, the turnkey came scuttling along the jail corridor, and opened the doors of the cells occupied by Hildreth and by Denny. In a manner ludicrously different from his former arrogance he said:

"Please come up to the courtroom, gentlemen."

"Son," reproved Denny, stepping out into the corridor, with Brant, "if you ever make so bold as to call me a 'gentleman' again, I'll sure have to push that pretty face of yours out from under your messenger-boy cap. I don't like to have muckers call me a gentleman. Someone might hear you and get to believing it."

" Sir, I —"

"Now what's the joke?" pursued Blayne. "Going to slap more bail onto us; or do we get shot at sunrise? Say, Brant, speaking of that, what walleyed idiot ever hit on the idee of shooting folks at sunrise? Sunrise is a bum time of day to get bumped off. Now if they'd wait till a guy had had his sleep out and had a nice breakfast and a once-over at the morning paper — say at about eleven o'clock —"

"Did you see who just came to the court-house?" Brant asked him, as they followed the turnkey along the short corridor and up a flight of stairs.

"I sure did. At least, I saw Groot and a —"

"That was Van Sluyk, the Supreme Court judge, with Groot," explained Hildreth. "I don't know what it means. Perhaps Groot is going to make a criminal libel charge against us, for that 'Seen in Sark' item of yours about him; now that we're already tied up on one such suit. If he is —"

"He ain't," declared Blayne, with much finality. "I know him a whole lot better than you do. He ain't here to make war medicine against us. He —"

"You know him better than I do?" queried Brant incredulously. "Nonsense. You never even met the man. You never saw him, except when you —"

"Nope?" cryptically replied Denny. "Didn't I? Brant, you know a lot. But you don't know everything."

The attendant reached a small closed door at the end of an upstairs hallway, and threw it wide, motioning the two prisoners to enter.

From boyhood memories, Hildreth knew it for the door leading to the county judge's private chambers, off the courtroom.

Van Sluyk and ex-Senator Groot were ensconced in the only two comfortable chairs in the little room; while Mayor O'Roon was hovering deprecatingly between them and assuring them at every other breath that County Judge Emerson Bogardus had been sent for and would be there in just a minute or so.

As Brant and Denny came into the room, O'Roon glanced at them in worried uncertainty as to how he should greet them. Very evidently the mayor had constituted himself host, in the absence of Coult and of Judge Bogardus. He was carrying off his duties with the easy grace of an elephantine jumping jack. Perturbation quivered in his every look and gesture. Sweat beaded his greasily fat face.

The "surprise visit" of a Supreme Court judge is, at best, a cause for commotion in any county courtroom. Just now, it had no auspicious aspects at all to Mayor O'Roon. The presence of the once-mighty and still-feared ex-Senator Groot did not add to any fragment of calmness which may have remained in O'Roon's cosmos.

Brant and Denny entered the room, and stood beside the door which the turnkey had closed behind them. Neither of them offered to speak. Even the irrepressible Blayne was stolidly, if alertly, silent.

It was Groot who relieved the situation. Heaving himself up from his chair with manifest difficulty, the ancient ex-senator hobbled across to where Hildreth stood. He laid both trembling clawlike hands on the younger man's broad shoulders; looking down on the compactly powerful figure with an almost fatherly affection.

"My boy," he said, "my very *dear* boy, will you accept the contrite apologies of an ill-tempered old man, for my abominable behavior the last time I met you? You received my unpardonable assault as I might have expected your gallant father's son to receive it."

"Sir!" babbled Hildreth. *"Sir!"*

Groot continued huskily:

"I can only say I did not understand. Mr. Blayne called on me, that same night. And he made it all clear to me. I would have come to you directly, then, with my humble contrition, had he not begged me to remain silent about his visit. This — this latest turn, I consider, has relieved me of the need of granting his plea. Will — will you shake hands, Brant, with a much shamed man to whom you are dear and to whom your father was like a loved son? I have no right to ask it, but —"

Hildreth checked the grotesquely stately appeal — which he did not find grotesque — by gripping the two bony hands in both his own, and exclaiming in a voice none too steady:

"Senator, you make me horribly unhappy

181

when you talk that way! If you'll just honor me with your friendship again, the whole thing is forgotten. I'm —"

The door flew open. County Judge Emerson Bogardus bustled in, puffing louder than usual and perspiring freely. His jet black beard wabbled like a goat's. Instantly, the softened expression was wiped from Derek Groot's face by a look of iron rigidity fraught with icy contempt more insulting than a kick.

Deliberately, he turned his back on the bowing and stammering young judge, and resumed his chair beside Van Sluyk. Bogardus scurried across to the Supreme Court jurist, greeting him with nervous effusiveness.

Chapter XXI

"Good afternoon, Judge," the older man cut in on Bogardus's welcome. "I happened to be visiting my friend, ex-Senator Groot, and I dropped in to see how things were going in your county. I find —"

"By your permission, Van," interposed Groot, with forensic dignity, "I beg to inform this young — this young person — of the actual facts. This morning, Bogardus, I received a telephone call from my friend, Mr. Dennis Blayne, here. (I understood him to say he was telephoning me without his partner's knowledge, and from a drugstore booth.) He told me of the impending arrest of Mr. Hildreth and himself on an egregious charge of criminal libel, and that they would be held, in all probability, on an iniquitously high bail. I telephoned at once to my friend and former colleague, Supreme Court Judge Van Sluyk. He was kind enough to drop his work at Trenton and to motor out to my home, where I told him the remaining details of the case, insofar as I had been able to glean them. Then we drove around here to call on you. That is all, Van," he concluded, turning courteously to his guest.

"Pardon my interruption. But this does not seem to me a time for circumlocution, nor for professional etiquette."

Van Sluyk smiled approval and understanding. Bogardus perspired still more freely, and mopped his wet forehead as he sought in vain for something fitting to say. His patron and mentor, Aschar Coult, was absent; on this one occasion above all others when the henchman needed sorely his help.

Denny Blayne's deferential courtroom stiffness of visage broke up in a grin of delighted appreciation of the scene's possibilities.

"I understand," resumed Van Sluyk, "I understand, Judge, that Messrs. Hildreth and Blayne, here, were brought before you this morning for preliminary hearing, on charges of criminal libel, and that you committed them for trial."

"Yes, Your Honor," babbled Bogardus, his throat suddenly pinched and inelastic. "On the evidence adduced, I had no option but to — Perhaps Your Honor would care to glance over the indictment? I have it here and —"

"Thanks," said Van Sluyk. "I should. And I —"

"And I am here," crackled Groot's parchment voice, "to go on these gentlemen's bail bond. A survey of the county clerk's records will show that my real and personal property, in this county alone, is far in excess of the exorbitant sum demanded. Therefore —"

"By the way, Judge," asked Van Sluyk, in elaborate ignorance, as Bogardus's trembling fingers exhumed the case's papers from a drawer, "what amount *did* you fix as their bail?"

"The sum," rasped Groot, before the flustered Bogardus could reply, "is twenty-five thousand for each of them."

"Twenty-five thousand dollars!" echoed Van Sluyk, with amazement even more elaborately expressed than had been his profession of ignorance as to the amount.

Then he laughed tolerantly.

"My dear Groot!" he exposulated. "Where is your old-time knowledge of legal procedure? Surely you must realize what a ridiculous thing you have just said. Two proprietors of a small rural newspaper, held by a learnéd county judge in such a preposterous sum as twenty-five thousand dollars apiece, on a mere charge of criminal libel! Now, if they were material witnesses or accomplices in a murder case, that bail might be barely possible. But never in a petty suit like this. Judge Bogardus, you must forgive the senator for repeating idle gossip he may have heard; and surely you yourself must see the humor of such a wild statement. By the way, what *is* the amount of their bail?"

As he asked the question he ran his eye over the sheaf of papers which Bogardus had placed obsequiously in front of him. He frowned, then smiled.

"Judge," said he, "I can't blame ex-Senator

Groot for misstating the amount so grossly. Even your own stenographer has made the same idiotic blunder. See — the record mentions the bail for each of the defendants as twenty-five thousand. I suggest you employ a more accurate court stenographer. For if such an erroneous record should reach Trenton it would react most seriously upon you. Now, what bail did you actually fix?"

"It seemed to me — it seemed — in view of the seriousness of the case — in view of the scurrilous nature — record — in view —" gobbled Bogardus, unsteadily — "it seemed —"

"Do you mean to say you *really* fixed their bail at twenty-five thousand each?" thundered Van Sluyk, his suavity changing with suspicious suddenness to judicial indignation. "You, a judge — sworn to administer the laws of this county and state according to the statutes — you held these two gentlemen in such an impossible sum? On a single unestablished charge of criminal libel? It is incredible!"

"I — I acted hastily, Your Honor," cringed Bogardus. "I can see that, now. I regret most deeply —"

"Perhaps, in view of your tardy clearness of vision," suggested Van Sluyk, drily, "you would care to change the amount named on the bail bonds?"

"Yes, Your Honor. Oh, yes, sir. By all means!" swiftly assented Bogardus. "Would — would one thousand dollars, each, seem to

Your Honor to be excessive? If so —"

"That is considerably better," coldly decreed Van Sluyk. "Here are the papers in the case. Suppose you make the change at once. I understand that ex-Senator Groot wishes to stand bondsman to them. I trust there is no objection to that, on the part of the court? Very good. Kindly have the matter attended to with as little delay as possible. I must start back to Trenton, directly. I am to speak there tonight. By the way, I shall have note made of the trial date, and I shall see that an authorized representative of the State Judiciary is here to report it for me. Kindly remember that — if you are still on the bench at the time."

"Brant," said Groot, "I want you and Blayne to dine with me, this evening, at seven-twenty, please. And now perhaps you would care to go out into the square and see some people who seem anxious as to your welfare. I think we can persuade Mayor O'Roon not to break up any peaceable demonstration which may occur there."

Dazedly, Brant Hildreth made his way out of the building and to the steps of the courthouse. The crowd was thicker than when last he had seen it. The man with the fountain pen and the envelope had been forced to borrow three more envelopes in order to write down all the names and pledged sums shouted by those around him.

Melvin was stepping down from the pedestal

of the war monument when he caught sight of Blayne and Hildreth descending the courthouse steps; alone and unguarded. His triumphant yell drew all eyes to him. Then he pointed ecstatically to the steps.

The rest was pandemonium.

There was a wild forward rush. The two released prisoners were caught up by a hundred eager hands and lifted high to willing shoulders. Thus they were borne above a madly cheering crowd toward the *Bugle* office.

This was the spectacle which seared itself into the unbelieving eyes of Aschar Coult, as the sheriff drove into the square on his way home from the Hudson.

The car well-nigh ran into a telephone pole, before its dumbfounded driver could remember to halt it. Coult stared goggle-eyed at the milling and laughing and cheering throng and at the two released prisoners who rode high on its shoulders.

Seven hours earlier, the sheriff had departed on his business trip, mightily content with the belief that he had crushed forever the partners and their pestilently aggressive newspaper and that Brant and Denny would spend at least a year in the cells; whence at last they would emerge stone-broke and discredited; the *Bugle* long since defunct.

Now, he returned to find the mass of Sark's population eddying joyously around its two heroes; the men Coult had believed were forever cleared from his path. It did not make sense to the flabbergasted sheriff.

Casting about in his mind for an explanation, he decided that the people had made up the bail amount, among them; though he did not understand how they had been able to do so. At once, his plan was formed. He would make Bogardus find a flaw in the bond, and he would have the prisoners rearrested and held in even higher bail.

His glance turned menacingly from the cheering mob to the courthouse where he reigned supreme. If Bogardus were not there, he should be sent for. The hand-picked judge was due for a merciless dressing down from his overlord for allowing the partners to go free on the combined payment of their bond; and for not declaring the form of payment illegal.

Aschar Coult's angry gaze focused on the courthouse, just in time to see Supreme Court Judge Van Sluyk and Groot descending the steps toward their waiting limousine, while a hatless and humbly bowing and cringing County Judge Emerson Bogardus escorted them meekly thereto. The sight told its own story.

At the same moment, someone in the crowd caught sight of the sheriff's familiar car, and of the sheriff himself seated statue-like in it. The huge police dog, Mowgli, sat vigilantly upright at Coult's side; the dog's wide morocco brass-studded collar shining in the sunset light.

There was a multiple groan and a sibilant sharpness of hissing. The irrepressible harelipped youth had returned to the square, unnoticed, and had mingled with the celebrants. Now, encouraged by the hisses and groans, he reached down for another of the ornamental whitewashed stones, and hurled it with much power and precision at the sheriff's gigantic figure.

The car's windshield was between the stone and its target. Into this sheet of thick glass the flung stone crashed. Glass fragments showered all over Coult and his dog. Mowgli growled furiously, springing to his feet and making as though to leap out of the machine and charge the entire crowd. But Coult's quick grip on the wide morocco collar forced the dog back.

And now there was no wholesale rebuke from the onlookers at the harelipped youth's stone-throwing. Indeed, several other young and irresponsible hangers-on stooped and groped on the ground among the forest of human legs, for missiles wherewith to continue the bombardment.

There was a general menacing surge of the whole assemblage toward the car where sat fearless and moveless the man they hated. A stone bounced off the fender. Another grazed Coult's broad-brimmed black felt hat.

Then through the looser volume of sound came Brant Hildreth's upraised voice, clarion clear; fierce in its hot authority.

190

"Back!" he trumpeted. "Let him alone! *Let him alone,* I said! Boys, are we going to spoil the very thing you're backing me up for doing? I'm working for law and order and cleanness in Preakness County. Are you going to wreck all that, by being as lawless as Coult himself? We'll put him out of business, fairly and squarely. Not by pitching onto him, a thousand to one."

At the imperative leadership of his words and tone, the onward surge slowed down to a shuffling standstill. Unobtrusively Aschar Coult slipped back into his pocket the black automatic pistol he held hidden in his lap.

"You boys started to take us to the *Bugle* office," continued Hildreth. "If you're tired, let us down and we'll walk. When we get there, I'm going to try to thank you for your faith in me and for your gorgeous friendship; if you'll let me talk to you for just a minute. Let's go!"

Toward Sussex Street swayed the crowd, amid renewed cries of "Speech! *Speech! SPE-E-ECH!*"

Chapter XXII

Aschar Coult was left unmolested, momentarily forgotten. Yet, long and motionless he sat there, in his car, beside the formidable dog and surrounded by splinters of windshield glass.

He did not heed a light cut or two which the flying fragments had inflicted upon his face and hands. He was staring after the departed crowd; his face bone white, his eyes clouded and brooding.

Not by chance had Aschar Coult risen to local greatness and wealth. Not by crass luck had he formed from unpromising material one of the strongest and most efficient political rings in the history of New Jersey, since the glowing era of "Staff" Little and of John Stockton and of Senator Dryden. The sheriff was a born leader, a born general, a born strategist; coldly unemotional; master of himself and of others.

Now, in a trice, he saw his power about to be stripped from him. He had been hissed and hooted and stoned, by the very people whom so long and so successfully he had despoiled. An outsider had come to Sark, and in a few short months had aroused the dormant majority of the county's decent citizens; the solid folk with whom the balance of power always rests. Hitherto these people had been too busy earning a living to dabble in politics. They had grumbled at the ring's rule, but they had not been scourged into action and they had had no leader to head a revolt.

If that leader could be done away with, there was time even yet for Coult to save the situation and to keep his own grip on the throats and the purse strings of the county. Lesser means had failed to oust Hildreth. Without Brant, his partner, Denny Blayne, would be a mere cipher, with no numeral in front of it. Brant was the one to get rid of. And the thing must be done quickly and with terrible effectiveness, or the people would become too wide awake to be drugged back to their chronic sleep.

Hildreth was the keystone of the new conditions. With him removed, the whole arch of revolt would crumble. Yet it must be done in such way as to cast no provable suspicions on Aschar Coult nor on his ring.

Gradually, the sheriff's head turned from the direction whence the crowd had disappeared. Gradually, his expressionless gaze rested on the soft bluish contour of the Ramapo Mountains beyond; the mountains wherein he had been born; the mountains whose half-wild Jackson White inhabitants he understood as can no outlander.

These mountaineers had grown to look on Aschar Coult as a demigod. He it was who guarded their moonshine distilleries from Federal discovery. He it was who sent them sure and timely warning of every raid planned against their fastnesses by searchers after illicit stills. He it was who had combined their scattered and warring whisky factions into one highly profitable body, and who had engineered the safe and lucrative sale of their raw moonshine products.

They were his adoring and blindly trusting tools — or at least enough of them for his present purpose.

Still ignoring the broken windshield and the glass abrasions on his tanned face and hands, Coult set his car in motion. He did not drive to the courthouse, nor to his tawdrily expensive new home. Instead, he guided the machine at top speed toward the distant crossroad which led directly up into the nearer accessible reaches of the mountains. The cloud of worry was gone from his wooden face. Once more he was in action — in deadly efficient action.

The cheering and enthusiastically friendly crowd had scattered at last from before the entrance of the little one-story *Bugle* building. Denny and Hildreth were left alone in the office they had quitted so forlornly that morning. They were tired, but they were supremely happy. Suddenly, Hildreth turned to his partner, shaking Blayne's wiry shoulder in mock wrath.

"You mangy faker!" cried Brant. "You said you were going over to the drugstore for some headache powders! And you really went there to send an S.O.S. call to ex-Senator Groot! Of all the crooked —"

"I got the headache powders, too," Denny defended himself. "Honest, I did, Brant. Three of 'em. I've never had a headache, but nobody can tell when I'm li'ble to. So it was a good thing to lay in a few powders. Besides —"

"Why didn't you tell me you were going to phone to Groot? I —"

"Because that would have spilled the whole works. You'd 'a' asked me how did I know him. And then I'd have had to tell you about me going to see him that night. And you had told me not to and not to do anything more about that 'Seen in Sark' thing I had wrote about him; and I knew you'd be sore and maybe give me another call down. So I kept my mug clamped shut, and I got the old feller to do likewise. He hadn't any call to squeal on me today, neither," finished Blayne, with an accent of grievance. "I've a good mind to get back at him by not going to his old mausoleum house to eat, tonight. I bet that'd peeve him, something turrible. He's —"

"Tell me about going there to see him," urged Brant. "Nobody's going to be sore at you, Denny, you white little cuss. Go ahead and tell me about it, won't you?"

Blayne fidgeted, as might a kindergarten child caught in a fault.

"Well," he began, hesitantly, "well, you see, I let on to be riled at the line of talk you gave me about that Santy Claus item I pulled on him. But all the time I could see I'd done you dirt. And I wished I had a third foot, so's I could kick myself. The big explosion of it was when I saw him whale you with that gold-roofed cane of his; and the way you took it and how you picked up his stick for him and helped him out to his carriage. That was one swat too much for Mrs. Blayne's handsome little son. So I asked where he lived, and that night I sneaked around there. I knew you'd give me blazes if you knowed about it. But I went."

He paused, to give dramatic effect to his narrative. Then he resumed:

"A stuffed-shirt butler person held me up at the door. I told him who I was and the paper I work on, and he said he'd see was Sen'tor Groot to home. (Say, Brant, that butler couldn't have treated me any more loving and cordial if I'd been a smallpox germ. Tonight, if he waits on us, I'm sure going to call him 'Feller!' or 'Me man' or 'Slobsy.' Just you see if I don't.)

"Well, presently he sasshays back from the lib'ry where he's gone to ask, and he comes out into the hallway and he says: 'Sen'tor Groot is not at home.' And I says to him: 'You frowzy

196

old cuttlefish, that's a lie from burning hell. I just heard him speaking to you. Leave me by.' I gives him just a little touch in the stomach with my elbow. While he's doubling up, I slips past into the lib'ry.

"There sits the old gentleman reading into a calf-bound lawbook. He glowers up at me, like I was the man who invented the income tax. Before he can order me out, I says: 'Listen, friend. It was me that wrote that squib about you in the paper. I wrote it because it was funny. Brant Hildreth never got a look at it till five minutes before you came there and hit him. That's Gawd's truth, Mr. Senator.' He tries to stop me once or twice, but I kept on at it. I says: 'Just before you come in there with your cane, I had showed him the piece. Why, Mr. Senator, Brant almost bust out a-crying when he read it. I thought he was going to lam my block off.

" 'Brant says to me, he says: "Blayne, I wouldn't 'a' had this happen, not if I had to lose my right arm, Blayne," says Brant Hildreth to me. "Blayne, Senator Derek Groot is the very greatest statesman Noo Jersey ever prodooced," says Brant to me. "And it was his example in pol'tics that fust give me the idee of starting this paper, to carry on his grand lifework," says Brant to me, Mr. Senator. And Brant says to me, furthermore: "Senator Derek Groot is the finest American since Abraham Lincoln. And I love him like he was my own father and I rev'rence him more'n anyone else on earth. And now look at the filthy way you've wrote about him! And I'll have to saddle the blame for it," says —' "

"Good Lord, Denny!" interrupted Hildreth, aghast. "I never said any of those crazy things, you little liar. You knew mighty well I didn't, and —"

"Yep," admitted Blayne, cheerfully, "*I* knew it, all right, all right. But old Groot didn't know it. Toplofty as he is, he swallered it, whole. He stopped trying to interrupt me; and he listens. And that old granite face of his begins to get real ca'm, not to say tickled. (The grandest of 'em ain't above believing nice things about themselves, you know.) And I goes on: 'Mr. Senator, after you'd gone away again, Brant turns to me and he says: "Blayne, it's no disgrace to be struck by a man like the senator; any more than for a child to be walloped by its dad. I'd rather be hit by him than shook hands with by most men, Blayne," says Brant to me. "But I'll never stop being heartbroke that such a grand man must go on believing I wrote such a libel about him — him being so handsome and noble-looking and all; and me just looking up to him like he was a emperor or something." ' "

"Denny!" gasped Hildreth.

"Then," continued Blayne, "I begun to eat dirt on my own account. I says to him: 'Mr. Senator, I had heard Brant speaking so wonderful about you, all this time, that I tried to

198

scrape acquaintance with you in the street. You high-hatted me. It made me mad. So I tried to think up all the untruest and impossiblest things I could say about the way you look. And that item was it. Now, you hit Brant with your cane when he didn't deserve it, Mr. Senator. He took it, sooner'n give me away, because he knew how ashamed I was, anyhow. There's the same cane, a-laying on your table. I want you should take it and give me the biggest thrashing I ever had. After that, I'll apologize to you for the lying item I wrote about you.'

"Well, I knew how it would tickle him to hear anyone talk that way. And I was right. He says: 'Let it pass. Your expl'nation is satisfactory. Now sit down, and tell me more about this campaign you and my old friend's son are planning.' Likewise, I done so. I stayed more'n an hour. When I came away, he says: 'I promise nothing, mind you. But it may be I can be of service to you, both, in my own way. I shall think it over, carefully, sir. Meanwhile, if ever you or Brant need personal assistance that is in my power to give, pray call on me.' Which same I done, this morning . . . Say, Brant, did I dream it or did I hear some lady talking to you in your cell?"

"No," corrected Hildreth, his eyes and voice suddenly wondrous soft. "You heard an angel. Not a lady. Hell's full of 'ladies.' A ministering angel, Denny. That's what you heard. As soon as you go back into the pressroom to melt up another batch of lead for the linotype — not that I want to hurry you — as soon as you go back in there and shut the door behind you, I'm going to call her up."

"Gee," mused Denny, plaintively, as he started for the back room. "Gee, but it's going to be rotten lonesome, being the only bachelor on all the *Bugle*'s staff! But a fine-looking and upstanding young chap, like me, hadn't ought to find it any great chore to catch me a bride, on my own account, if I get too lonesome. Most any girl would be glad to team up with a splendid sweet-souled guy like me."

Chapter XXIII

The door slammed on his unfinished soliloquy, and Brant Hildreth picked up the desk telephone. A servant's voice, at the Cormick house, answered the call. Brant asked to speak with Miss Cormick, giving his name. A minute later, came the servant's prim reply:

"Mr. Cormick says his sister doesn't wish to speak with you, sir. And he asks that you will not telephone his house again."

It was an awed Denny Blayne, despite his best clothes and his habitual assurance, who followed Hildreth into the dim old living room of ex-Senator Derek Groot's dim old house, an hour or so later. With the help of his cane, Groot arose heavily to his feet and moved forward to welcome his two guests.

He was in irreproachable evening dress, a costume as quaint and ancient in its way as were his daytime frock coat and bell-crowned hat. Brant himself scarce felt at ease in this atmosphere of sixty years agone. He looked forward to a drearily stupid evening for all of them.

The stiff formality of the dinner itself bore

out his worst fears. In vain his own spasmodic efforts at conversation and Groot's stately contributions to table talk sought to lift the dullness of the meal.

For a space, Denny sat wordlessly on the edge of his chair, eating almost nothing and handling the unaccustomed silver and thin glass and porcelain as if they had dynamitic potentialities.

At last the prolonged silences, punctuated only by a quarter-occasional dull phrase of civility from their host or from Brant, began to get on the little East-sider's nerves. That, and the forbidding environment and the strangeness of it all. Racking his puzzled brain for a congenial theme of discourse, he found one. He launched into a spasmodic attempt at conversation, only to realize presently that he was conducting a monologue.

"At that," he began, apropos of nothing at all, "I doubt if Friend Aschar Coult ever sees the inside of a cell. No matter what we get on him. There's a swad of folks that just naturally never has to pay their bill, no matter how big that bill may be. I think Aschar Coult's one of them. We can prove all sorts of things against him. And that's all the harm it's li'ble to do him . . . Then again, there's folks who can't so much as pick up a plugged nickel off'n the sidewalk without getting into a jam with the law."

He paused for breath. Neither of his hearers picked up his conversational lead. Silence settled, more stifling than ever. Doggedly, Blayne made a second and more strenuous struggle to smash through it.

"F'r instance," he expounded, "Larry Katrine told me a funny thing about that. Larry worked on the old *Chronicle*, back in Noo York, Senator, along with Brant here and me. You'll remember Larry, Brant?"

"In the cut room, wasn't he?" asked Hildreth, with no interest at all. "Yes, I remember him."

Denny Blayne drew a deep breath. The going was heavy and heavier. But he set his prognathous jaw and stuck to his task of demolishing the thick silence.

"Larry said he used to live in a little burg down in Pennsylvania or Delaware or Maryland or somewheres," he plodded on. "I forget which. Anyhow it wasn't Noo York, nor yet Jersey. And I forget the name of the burg, too. It's hard to remember. You see, Senator, all those rube towns have different names."

"So I have heard," assented Groot, thus directly appealed to.

"Well," continued Denny, fiercely resolved to keep the leaden conversational ball rolling, "Larry told me about two fellers who lived down there. I forget their monickers, too, and it don't matter. Let's give one of 'em the quaint Oriental name of Smith. Let's stretch our 'maginations into calling the second one Jones.

"Smith is a truck driver. His wife dies, and he's left with nobody but their kid son that they both thought the world of. On top of that, he's laid off, on account of times was hard. He's lost his wife and he's lost his job."

Another pause which nobody broke, until Blayne forged ahead:

"So Smith gets drunk. Like a lot of us, he got drunk for what he hoped to forget. Not for what he was hoping to get. He wasn't a drinking man, as a rule. He was driving the truck, on his last trip with it before he was to be dropped from the job. And he's so drunk he runs it past a red light and into the mayor's car. Which same he busts up, along with the truck.

"They arrested him; and they left him in the cells to sleep it off. I figger he woke up, before daylight, and got to remembering his wife was dead and his job was gone and he was in the cooler and that he had disgraced his little son by the stunt he had pulled. There didn't seem to be anything ahead for him. So he rigs up a kind of rope, with his suspenders and his pants, and he gets onto his cot and he ties the rope to the water pipe that runs along the ceiling. They found him hanging there, stone dead . . . So much for Smith and for the bill he pays for one sample-size spree."

"A cheery dinner story," commented Hildreth, as Blayne paused for effect.

"Yep, isn't it?" agreed Denny. "Quite a sad change from the jolly line of chitchat we've been tossing around the table, ever since we set down to eat."

Blayne's East-side dander was up. Rebukes or no rebukes, he was going to finish his recital.

"Now we come to Jones, the other chap," he snapped, glowering from one to the other of his unresponsive listeners. "Jones was the big man of that town. Law and insurance and such. He was on the boards of all its half-handful of companies. He was a director of its misses'-and-children's-size bank. And he was in state politics, too. He was a back-slapper and an all-round good feller and educated and a lender and a nice generous spender. The town's noos-paper ate out of his hand, like its name was Fido. And he had a big underground pull. A sort of Maryland-or-Pennsylvania-or-Delaware Aschar Coult."

Denny paused, this time less hopefully. Then he meandered on, his annoyed brows ever blacker:

"Well, Jones milks all the companies he's in. And what he doesn't do to the bank would have been news to Jesse James. Likewise what he done to some trust funds. While he is pyra-miding his winnings on Wall Street, the De-pression crawls into view. Jones is wiped out, in the Market. The bank is cleaned out, and has to put up the shutters. Jones's companies is cleaned out. So is the whole little town. Every-body is broke. That burg is sure split wide open and starving. Jones is indicted. He demands a jury trial — which same he never gets to — and he slams all the blame for his crookedness onto a banker who has just died. You see, in his day of need, Heaven sends Jones a corpse to take the rap.

"The town was ten years in getting out of the red.

"When Jones dies in his sleep at last, what do the folks in that burg do? Do they yank him out of his thousand-dollar casket and nail his crooked skin to the nearest latrine door? They do not. They have his body lying in state in the Borough Hall for three days, all banked with enough floral tributes to stink up a whole cemetery. Everybody turns out, crying, to his funeral. They bury him under a monument half as big as the Woolworth Building. And the selectmen vote to name a Civic Center after him.

"In the pauper corner of that same cemetery, by the way, poor Smith has been pottersfielded. Him who hanged himself. Larry told me Smith is still used as a Horrible Example, by Sunday-school teachers down there. And Jones's memory is still worshiped by the crowd of folks he broke.

". . . I figger Aschar Coult will be a second Jones; no matter how hard we put him over the jumps. Small town folks are queer. That's their chief likeness to big town folks, I guess."

His voice trailed away. Senator Groot got up from his carved chair, with the help of his butler, as a signal that no dinner really is endless. He led the way, shamblingly, to the library. The disgruntled Denny brought up the rear.

There, coffee was served. There, too, Groot proceeded to make up for any lack of liveliness that had gone before. For he took from his table a long envelope and handed it to Brant.

"Take it," said he. "This will save me the trouble of having it mailed to you as usual. It is my life rule never to talk business during meals."

Hildreth puckered his eyes in unbelieving astonishment as he noted the envelope's vaguely familiar superscription. Then he opened the envelope itself and drew forth a single-typed page of legal size, in the form of a letter. It was signed in typewriting, "Old Roman."

"It — it is *you* who have been sending the *Bugle* these 'Old Roman' letters?" babbled Hildreth, staring agape at his drily smiling host. "YOU?"

"Why not?" asked Groot. "I owed you something for my violence and injustice toward you. And I owed the community something. It has been a privilege to help you on in your fight to better our county."

"But, Senator —"

"Years ago, I dropped out of politics. They grew too complex and too unclean for me, as I aged and weakened. And as the world changed and left me behind. But I have used my brain and my many reliable sources of local information, as steadily as ever. For my own entertainment, I have made many notes and have secured and docketed the proofs to substantiate them. After Mr. Blayne's visit to me, some weeks ago, it occurred to me I might crystallize my information into a series of letters to your paper. I did so."

"But why didn't you sign them, sir? Or at the least why didn't you let me know you were their author? If you had done that, I should have printed them without so much as troubling to verify a single statement. I —"

"I did not sign them," the precise and dust-dry old voice returned, "because it has never been my custom to write for the press. Doubtless, journalism is a worthy and even a noble profession. But a statesman — according to my perhaps antiquated ideas — lowers himself when he dabbles in any profession but his own."

"But if you had let me know the letters were written by you, you surely could have trusted me to keep your secret," urged Hildreth, while Denny sat with surprise-widened eyes and mouth. "I should have —"

"I know you would, my very dear lad," answered Groot. "But how could I tell what your reaction would be, toward communications written by a man who had tried to flog you? You might well have been petty enough — or human enough — to tear them up, unread. So I told no one . . . They seem to have had some slight effect on the opinions of the community," he finished, half-deprecatingly.

"Some slight effect?" repeated Brant. "Why,

Senator, they have been bombshells! They have been the backbone of our entire campaign. I can never thank you enough, sir! And you will continue them? I pledge my word and Blayne's that nobody shall suspect their authorship."

"I shall be glad to continue them," promised Groot, in evident gratification at the astonished delight of his guests. "I still have plenty more material. And I shall hold you to your joint promise of silence as to who writes them, only so long as you are not called to account, legally, for any of their statements. If ever such time comes, you are released from your pledge. I shall announce myself as the author of the 'Old Roman' letters, and I shall bring to court full proofs of every word I have written in them. Be assured of that."

Brant's eye was running down the long sheet's close-typed contents.

"H'm!" he commented. "Tackling the road graft again, eh? And specializing on the new Hudson-Preakness Highway! That road is the pride of the courthouse gang. They point to it as a perfect bit of work, whenever they are criticized for anything else. This'll stir up a sweet rumpus!"

"I have a copy of the contract specifications, on that road," said Groot, "and a certified copy of the county board's report that all the specifications have been fulfilled. Here are the two copies. Keep them. Today, I took the liberty of using my slight influence with Judge Van Sluyk to help us on a plan of mine. He will arrange that the State Road Board's boring machine is to be sent here next Saturday, at noon — about three hours after the *Bugle* is on the street — to test the road in several places."

"*After* it is on the street? But that —"

"That will enable you to announce its coming, in the *Bugle*, three hours in advance. It will give the people time to gather to witness the boring. But it will not give Coult's satellites time to do anything in the way of improving or changing the road. Van Sluyk will see that inspectors are sent with the machine who are wholly honest and reliable. An expert will be sent along, with apparatus for testing the borings as soon as they are made. The tests will be made in the presence of the townsfolk and the report will be announced to them."

"Great!" exclaimed Hildreth; but Denny looked puzzled.

"What kinds of tests?" asked Blayne.

"I saw some made in the Bronx, when I was a reporter," explained Brant. "The state has a machine with a boring instrument at the end of it. It's fastened to a truck. The borer cuts a core about five inches in diameter out of any part of the road that the inspectors may order to be 'tapped.' The core proves what material has been used and if it is the specified depth, and all that. If the expert is along, as Senator Groot says he's to be, he can make tests in five minutes that will show whether the concrete is of the specified strength or not. We'll copy his report and run it alongside this table, of specifications as to material and depth."

"Ralph Cormick is chairman of the Board of Freeholders, too!" chuckled Denny, as he began to understand. "If they've put bum stuff or short-depth stuff on the road, it'll be a nice pickle for him."

"Cormick does what Aschar Coult tells him to," said Groot. "I doubt if the young man has the slightest idea of many of the things he is made to do. But Mr. Blayne is right. It will give Cormick a black eye. It will come close to ruining his political future, if the tests prove dishonesty."

Of a sudden, Brant Hildreth's first glow of enthusiasm for the road-testing scheme ebbed. He tried to revive his long-ago zest in the thought that his exposure of Preakness County corruption would be an honestly struck blow at Ralph Cormick, and would punish in part his own early grievances at Cormick's hands. He reminded himself of Cormick's insulting behavior toward him since his return to Sark; a series of affronts culminating with Ralph's brutally forbidding message transmitted to him over the telephone that same afternoon.

But somehow, Hildreth could not stir up within himself the desired angry satisfaction at thought of harming this enemy of his. Between him and his revenge drifted a winsome little bronzed face. In his ears echoed with faint sweetness a voice pleading:

"Won't you please forgive me? Please, *please* do, Brant! I'm so ashamed! Won't you be friends again? I CAN'T have you stay in this hideous place!"

Kay had fulfilled the Biblical command to "visit the prisoner." She had done more. She had wanted to risk her half of the Cormick house and all her own money in going bail for him, that he might be freed from his cell. And now, he was arranging to ruin her brother!

Again and again Brant told himself that Ralph was doing his ferocious best to ruin Hildreth and Denny. He told himself Cormick was part of Coult's gang which was bleeding the county white and was making its fair fame a mockery.

Yet, ever his thought came back to the girl who must suffer, in pride if in no other way, through her brother's disgrace. And he began to hate his self-chosen role of reformer.

Well did he realize there could be no turning back, now that his hands were set to the work.

His duty was to the community which had grown to trust him; to the men who, that day, had sought to pool their scanty assets in an effort to bail him. For the sake of these and of his duty he must antagonize once more — this time forever — the woman for whom he would right blithely have laid down his tired life.

With an effort he wrenched his mind away from its miserably brooding introspection, and

212

forced himself to listen to his host.

"It is only fair to warn you both," the measured old tones were saying, "that there is a far greater peril in this campaign of yours than either of you may realize. The ring — the gang — whatever you may choose to term it — is the mere impotent weapon of Aschar Coult. Without him it is nothing and less than nothing. Without him, it would resolve itself at once into its former useless and innocuous handful of individual nonentities."

"He —"

"It is Coult who has welded the county ring. It is Coult who not only holds it together but makes it terribly potent for evil. Coult is perhaps the most remarkable man, in his own way, in all my long life's observation of men. He has strange genius. He is without conscience. He is without fear. He will stick at nothing. I am astonished at the mild methods to which he has confined himself, thus far, in dealing with you. But you are pushing his back closer and closer to the wall. When he can retreat no further — *look out for him.*"

Chapter XXIV

"What d'ye mean, look out for him?" queried Blayne. "Ain't we —"

"I mean that he will not stop short of murder," said the old man, solemnly. "I mean he will try to kill you both — Brant especially — if he believes you are vitally dangerous to him. He will kill you, if he can. And he will do it in such way that the blame cannot be brought home conclusively to him. He cares for but one thing — one person — on earth. And that one is Aschar Coult. He will have no mercy on anybody who stands between him and success. Least of all, on anyone who stands between him and safety. You are cutting away his chances of continued success. Presently, you will be cutting away his chances of safety. Prison will loom before him. If he can save himself by killing you, he will do it."

"He —"

"I am not an alarmist. But I offer you this warning most earnestly. When he strikes, you will not know it is he who is striking. Indeed, the chances are that you will never again know anything. Be on your guard. You in particular, Brant. Mr. Blayne is in much less danger. For without you he cannot make the paper what it has grown to be. Do you go armed, either of you? I hope so."

"Nope," dissented Blayne. "Me, I've never toted a gun, nor yet a knife; though I was brought up in the middle of a neighborhood where kids cut their teeth on 'em. Somehow, I never could get the hang of lugging an arsenal. The straight left to the jaw was always good enough for me. And maybe a butt in the stomach, if I was ganged."

"I did a bit of boxing and football and mat work in college," said Brant, as the inquiring old eyes shifted to him. "And I've kept myself in condition ever since. I never saw the need of carrying a pistol."

"That's the lad's silly way of saying he's maybe the best rough-and-tumble scrapper and the toughest-muscled guy the noospaper profession ever had in it, Mr. Senator," expounded Denny. "Muldoon said if Brant had took to the ring he'd have made most of the crop of noo heavyweights look like they was a piece of cheese. Nope, Brant don't need no gun. He don't need nothing but an even break, when Old Man Trouble drops in on him. He —"

"Nevertheless," protested Groot, "I should be better satisfied if both of you went armed. It is no concern of mine," he added, looking at his watch, and rising painfully from his deep chair.

"And now," he said, "I am going to ask you

young men to excuse me. I am ninety-two years old, you know. Physically, in my second childhood, Dr. Vreeland tells me. And he says no child should be allowed to sit up after nine o'clock at night. His orders are very strict. And I have disobeyed them already, by more than twelve minutes. Good night, to both of you. Thank you for taking pity on an old man's loneliness this evening. And remember, I am with you, heart and soul, in this campaign of yours. My 'Old Roman' letters are always at your service. So is such slight political influence as I still may wield by proxy. So are my financial resources. Good night, Mr. Blayne. Good night, Brant, my very dear boy."

He tottered to the front door with them. He stood there, framed in the lamplight, watching them go down the walk. Brant turned at the gate and waved good-by to him. The clawlike old hand was waved back to him in a gesture that was almost a benediction.

Early next morning a manservant went into Groot's bedroom, as usual, to awaken him. The elongated thin form lay moveless under its heavy coverlet. On the classic old face was the ghost of a smile.

Very quietly, very peacefully, ex-Senator Derek Groot had died in his sleep. The hurriedly summoned physician said it might well have happened at any time during the past three years. For the worn-out heart had long been a broken-down tenant of the worn-out body.

News of Groot's death came to the two partners as they reached the *Bugle* office for the day. Both were keenly shocked by the tidings. Denny was the first to rally.

"Say," he observed, "now we'll have to keep on holding our tongues, for always, about who 'Old Roman' was. We —"

"I had thought of publishing this last letter of his," said Brant, "with a black line around it; and I thought I'd write an editorial telling the whole story and letting the county people know how much they're indebted to him for his splendid help in exposing corruption and —"

"Gee!" snorted Denny. "Man alive, come *out* of it! Use the brains — if any — that the good Lord gave you. What's kept Coult from suing us for libel, on the things in those 'Old Roman' letters? Why, because he thought they were wrote by some squealer in his own crowd who had gave us proofs of everything he claimed. Well, then, s'pose you tell the cock-eyed world who 'Old Roman' was? S'pose you say them letters was all wrote by a man who's dead and who can't back a single word he wrote in 'em. Hey? How about it? What does Friend Coult do, if you lay yourself wide open like that?"

"I —"

"Groot is dead — Lord rest him!" pursued

Blayne. "And all them proofs of his is dead, along with him. So is all the help he offered us. It's all out. OUT. Why, we'll be playing in crazy good luck, you and me, if Coult don't get wise to who it was, in another couple of weeks, when he don't see any more 'Old Roman' letters in the *Bugle*! Spill the beans, by telling who it was, would you? You're cuckoo, Brant. That's what you are. Cuckoo. Don't bad luck travel our way fast enough, without you giving it an extry shove?"

"You're right!" admitted Hildreth. "You're dead-right. It would upset everything, if I told. No, we'll have to keep it secret forever, now. I was a fool not to think of that. This next 'Old Roman' letter — the one about the rotten roads — will be published, just as the others have been. It will be another week before anyone but ourselves will know the series is ended. Perhaps nobody will guess who wrote them, even when they stop. . . . By the way, here's a notice from the freight office that that batch of casting lead has come. Better send a truck for it."

"All right. That means a nice happy evening for me, after the reg'lar work's cleared away. If there's one part of this bum job of mine that I love well enough to kiss it, it's the chore of melting up lead all evening, for typecasting. When drops of it don't spatter out and burn holes in me, the ladle turns in my hand. And I have to drop it and yank off a spoiled pair of brogans before the hot stuff eats through the leather and puts my feet out of business. Yep, lead-melting is a gladful stunt, all right. Gives me something to look forward to, all the bright busy day."

Turning a deaf ear to his partner's chronic grumbling, Hildreth settled himself to the writing of ex-Senator Groot's obituary. But he was in no mood for the sad task. Twice he tore up what he had written. He was nervous. Street noises bothered him, unwontedly. A stream of people filtered into the office on petty business of their own or else to congratulate him loudly on his release from jail.

At last, Hildreth gave up the effort to write the obituary as he wished it written. He resolved to come back to the office, in the evening, when the street should be quieter and visitors less likely to come in; and when he could work undisturbedly at this last tribute to his father's old friend.

Accordingly, behind down-drawn shades that night, the lights burned brightly in the front office where Brant was adding the finishing touches to the Groot obituary; and in the pressroom at the rear where Denny Blayne was busy at his abhorred duty of melting lead for the linotype machine.

Blayne's continuous undertone of complaint, and his occasional explosions of blasphemy when a redhot drop of lead grazed him, had annoyed Hildreth into shutting the door leading into the rear of the shallow little building. The door was thin, but it kept out at least part of the volume of grouchy sound.

At Hildreth's feet drowsed Thane.

The deserted street silences were broken by a low sound which registered almost unnoted upon Brant's hearing. It was a very soft multiple shuffle, as of unshod human feet. It ceased, as Hildreth became consciously aware of it. Followed an instant of sibilant whispers.

Then, with startling suddenness, Thane woke from his nap and sprang up growling. Before he could take a step forward, the front door was opened. In through the aperture, noiseless and swiftly, surged a dozen rough-clad men. In an incredibly short time they had debouched in from the street, and had closed the door behind them, slipping the bolt.

They seemed to fill the small office. Well did the astonished Hildreth recognize their type. These were unquestionably a party of Jackson Whites, from the recesses of the Ramapo Mountains to eastward — uncouth, savage, half-drunk and wholly determined.

Thane launched himself ragingly at them. The foremost man of the group caught the leaping dog deftly by the throat — at the expense of a deep-furrowed gash in the right hand — and hurled him with Titan force against the nearest wall. The collie's head smote against the wainscot edge. He tumbled inert and limp to the floor.

Brant had sprung at the intruders as swiftly

and as furiously as had Thane. They closed in around him; avid, lethally noiseless.

To the floor he crashed, under a mountain of murderous humanity; his splendid strength cramped and rendered useless by sheer weight and numbers.

A curved knife glinted above his dizzy eyes. Horny bare feet kicked at his face. Hands with vise-fingers were busy at his throat. Men pounced on his muscular arms, pinioning them and his legs to the floor boards.

Chapter XXV

From the moment when Thane's challenge and the office front door's silent opening apprised Brant Hildreth of the inrush of the Jackson Whites, to the moment when his dog lay in a supine huddle in the room corner and he himself was buried beneath the wave of charging men, not five seconds in actual time had elapsed.

The surprise attack had been a complete success. This was no chance rabble of mountaineer rowdies, fighting drunk and mischievous, who had chosen Hildreth casually as victim for roughhousing.

Brant knew enough of the Jackson Whites to realize, in the first instant of attack, that these were picked men and that a prearranged plan of battle actuated them.

The average Ramapo mountaineers are narrow-chested and of no great physical prowess. But among them is to be found here and there a genuine giant for strength and savagery; formidable in rough-and-tumble warfare, bestially fearless.

The dozen hillbillies who had stormed the *Bugle* office were of this type. Picked men, they; carefully chosen for the purpose on which they had descended from their hill fastnesses; and very evidently coached as to their method of overcoming Hildreth in a concerted rush before he could do anything to guard against the onslaught. Even Thane's dash at them, in his master's defense, had been foreseen and cleverly blocked.

In old-fashioned storybooks alone can the most accomplished athlete hold his own against a dozen or even a half-dozen determined assailants. In real life he has not the ghost of a chance against such numbers.

True, as he met the rush, Brant's left fist had been driven thuddingly into the nearest unshaven face, with a piston force that sent a mountaineer to hands and knees spitting forth broken teeth. A viciously scientific right swing had smitten flush upon the chin of a second assailant, dislocating the jaw and dropping the jaw's owner to the floor in brief unconsciousness.

But those two lightning-quick blows were the only form of counter-attack Hildreth had scope to launch before the human whirlwind was upon him, dragging him down and clinging to his arms and his legs.

To the floor he crashed, the mound of Jackson Whites piling up on him as players might pile on a tackled runner in a football game.

Under those many hundreds of pounds of crushing weight, Brant writhed helplessly.

With trained and prearranged accuracy, they threw and held him. By the time he touched the floor — strangled, hard-held, impotent — a razor-keen knife with a crooked blade was thrust forward from somewhere in that welter of innumerable arms. It was poised for an instant above his heaving throat as though for greater accuracy of aim.

Brant shut his eyes. Then, ashamed of his own mental shrinking, he opened them again. Steadily he looked upon his impending death.

Well did he know who had sent these men hither; and why. The campaign was ended, so far as Hildreth was concerned. It had been a good fight, all these months, and, though he himself must die, he knew the Cause he had fought for would live.

Vaguely he wondered at Denny's sane caution in remaining out of the way at such a time; Denny who loved a rough-and-tumble battle for its own sake and who was as devoid of fear us any Irish terrier.

Blayne must have heard the rush and Thane's challenge growl and the ensuing crash of bodies to the creaking floor. He must have heard and understood. But also he must have realized his own inability to cope with such a mass of assailants. Apparently, he had chosen the sane course, and had slipped out of one of the rear windows and run for help.

Small chance would Blayne have for rousing any member of Sark's tiny police force! Coult would have arranged that the police should be on duty elsewhere than in this particular neighborhood at the time of the attack.

In the merest eye-flicker did all this flash through the helpless man's brain; even while the knife steadied itself and poised for its lethal throatslash. Then —

Behind him and above him resounded an ear-cracking screech — such a maniac war yell as might issue from the combined lungs of ten Apaches or a score of rabid wildcats.

A hideous and deafening and compelling noise it was; shrill, raucous, terrifying. It filled the crowded room like the hoot of a steam calliope. It seemed to sound from the upper air.

The Jackson Whites heard it. They knew it issued from none of their own number; they who had been enjoined to complete silence. One or two of them, at the rear of the close-packed mass, turned instinctively to see whence it came. Then, as an echo to it, resounded their own cries of horror — cries which drew the attention of the rest of the half-human wolf pack.

All at once, amid the babel, Brant Hildreth felt the intolerable strangling pressure lifted from him. The knife vanished. The Jackson Whites were easing their onslaught. Tucking his legs under him, Brant rolled sharply to one side; shielding his head with his arms.

None stayed him in his twisting shift from

under the dissolving welter of bodies. He rolled again, in practically the same motion, and reeled to his feet.

Once more, none hindered nor molested him, nor seemed to note his escape from the bottom of the warring pyramid. No longer was it a pyramid. It had changed to a shrinking and gaping huddle of fear-struck men, edging backward toward the door, their bulging eyes all converging in dumb panic upon one spot.

The room was hazy with stirred-up dust. Through the murk, Hildreth saw Denny Blayne.

Denny crouched atop the center table. He was stripped to the waist. Sweat poured from him. His swart simian face was distorted with fury. In one hand he held a metal pot which smoked and flamed and simmered. In the other fist he brandished a long-handled ladle; brimming with molten lead.

No diagram was needed, to tell the most ignorant of the Jackson Whites the meaning and the horrible menace of what they saw. From babyhood they had seen lead melted for bullet molds. From babyhood they had known the intolerable anguish caused by a chance drop of the leaden fire falling on human flesh.

Here was a gallon pot of the awful stuff. Here too was a pint ladle, full of it — a ladle which swung in air, as if about to launch its blinding and torturing contents into their blanched faces.

Small wonder that these ordinarily fearless mountain men shrank back from the wordless threat! It is one thing to face possible death from gun or knife — both of which may well miss any vital spot. It is quite another thing to stand unmoved in the path of a shower of molten lead; which can cut through the thickest clothing and can sear the eyeballs into eternal sightlessness.

The Jackson Whites huddled back toward the door. In another instant they would break and run, crowding and shoving one another mercilessly aside in their crazed efforts to escape out into the safety of the deserted black street, before the stream of fiery torment could be flung into the thick of them.

But Denny Blayne would not have it so.

"Over into that corner!" he shrilled, dancing up and down in maniac fury on the table top. "Over into that corner! The first man that takes a step nearer the door gets this whole thing in his face. *Move,* you snaggle-toothed swine of hell! *Jump,* I'm telling you!"

Over their heads flew a ladleful of melted lead. It splashed against the frame of the door. Much of it spattered out into the room. Stray drops of it flicked back against the heads and bodies of those nearest the entrance. They cringed from it; howling, as the points of fire stung them like hornets.

Denny had refilled his ladle from the pot, in the fraction of a second. Again the ladle was poised on high. Again echoed the snarlingly shrill command:

"*Into that corner*, I said!"

This time there was no hesitance. None dared risk the barrage of molten flame which already had deluged the door top. Shuffling, cursing, sniveling, they milled and jostled toward the far corner. With upraised ladle, Denny herded them thither, moving the ladle ever so little in the direction of such few of them as hesitated to obey his shrieked command.

"Stand there!" he yelled, flecks of foam on his thin lips. "Stand there! And *keep* standing there! If one of you mangy she-mongrel's litter moves so much as a step, I'll start baptizing the lot of you. And I won't let up till there's a gallon of lead-fire eating into your stinking carcasses. It'll be time enough, then, to finish what's left of you, with my gun. Stand quiet! And hands *up!* Keep 'em UP!"

To emphasize further his orders, Blayne scattered a half-ladleful of the streaming lead along the floor just in front of the human huddle. It cut into the hard boards. A score of tiny drops rebounded searingly against the feet and trouser legs of the foremost of the group. The prisoners yelping, clumped closer together into a tight bunch, in their corner. His eyes still fixing them, and his ladle poised, Denny commanded:

"Brant! Get to the phone. These poor goofs

won't have had the wit to cut the wires. Call up the state troopers' station. Not the Sark Police Headquarters. Cady and his bums will be picking huckleberries, just now, ten miles from here. And they'd turn these skunks loose, anyhow, even if they did arrest them. Call up the troopers. They're square. Tell Crayne to bring all the men in the station, and to bring them on the run! Hustle!"

There was a movement and a mutter among the cowed mountaineers, at mention of the dreaded New Jersey state police. Another half-dipper of lead, laid down as a barrage between them and the door, sent them cowering back into close formation.

Brant was at the telephone, before Denny's instructions were half voiced. As the Jackson Whites still milled and cringed and swore, he began to give Sergeant Crayne, at the far end of the wire, a curt outline of the situation.

Hildreth finished his message and hung up the receiver. His gaze fell on the corn-colored collie he loved. The great dog was huddled, where he had fallen, against the wall. Brant's blood went as hot as the molten lead itself, at memory of Thane's gallantly useless effort to save him, and at the fate that had been meted out to the hero dog. His heart was heavy within him, as he took a step toward his sacrificed chum.

A shiver ran through the inert mass of fur. Slowly, waveringly, Thane lifted his beautiful head. He peered, blinking about him.

His skull had banged resoundingly upon the wainscot edge, as the Jackson White had hurled him against the wall. The impact had stunned the collie, even as a jaw punch might stun a trained pugilist. But the shock was passing off. And, as with a knocked-out pugilist, the toughly healthy constitution of the young dog was throwing aside the effects of the blow.

Wabblingly, Thane got to his feet. He swayed a little on his braced legs, as he stared dizzily around him. His gaze centered on the huddle of rough men in the corner. The watchdog-instinct seeped back into play, at the sight. His upper lip curled, showing a glint of shining white eyetooth. His hackles bristled. Deep down in his furry throat an angry growl was born.

He took a lurching step toward the massed intruders. Then, through the buzzing in his brain, came his master's call:

"Thane! *Back!* Come here and lie down."

His head rapidly clearing and the co-ordination between brain and muscles beginning to re-establish itself, the collie obeyed. Slowly, reluctantly, he came back to where Brant Hildreth stood beside the desk. Brant's hand caressed the collie's bruised scalp, seeking for possible fracture. The dog curled up, obediently, at his feet.

There Thane lay, his deep-set dark eyes fixed in wrathfully perplexed disapproval at the clump of outlander men for whose presence in the sacred office he could not account. Once in a while, he looked up questioningly into Hildreth's face, then resumed his watch of the prisoners.

Already the dog was himself again. There was a bruise on the side of his head. But Brant's gently exploring fingers proved the skull itself had not been harmed. For the rest, Thane was none the worse for his brief senselessness. Moreover, he was highly entertained at the inexplicable scene before him. He could not understand any of it. But his psychic collie instincts told him the room was vibrant with mad emotion. Human excitement was food and drink to Thane's drama-loving soul.

Chapter XXVI

Denny continued to poise his ladle; every now and then checking an incipient attempt of one or another of his captives to bolt for the door by tensing his ladle-arm as if for a fling of the molten horror.

"My little friends," he orated, "when Sheriff Aschar Coult sicked you onto this pretty stunt, he told you he'd see you didn't get into any trouble over it. Likewise he told you he'd pay you good for the job. Well, you see just what Friend Aschar's promises are worth, in U.S. currency. Because you're in a peck of trouble, right now. And you're due to stay in trouble. And Aschar Coult can't pry you loose from it. Likewise he can't pay you the cash he promised you. Because you won't be there to get your pay."

He balanced his ladle afresh. Then he resumed his homily:

"Take this tip from your Uncle Denny, my friends: Aschar Coult is a dud. He's all wet. Washed up. His day is over, in this county and everywhere else. He was grand, when he had it. But he's a dead one now. So dead he stinks. Too dead to skin. Them that pins their hopes to Coult are pinning 'em to a snowball in hell. He —

"Git back there, you! *You,* — you pretty pustule with the buck teeth and the ingrowing forehead. It's YOU I'm meaning, son! That's the second time I've saw you try to edge out at one side, like you was aiming for the door. Next time, you'll get a pint of nice burning lead on your bean, for a shampoo. Just to delouse you. I ain't going to warn you again — Nor *you,* either, you with the face that hasn't got any teamwork and the eyes that ain't mates. You with the checked shirt. Your face'd look a heap nicer, with a pretty pattern of lead biting into it. Your own unmarried mother wouldn't even recognize you. And that's what it's due to have if you stir again."

He raised the ladle, as if to cast its contents at the group. The cursing and whimpering burst forth in renewed volume. The men jostled each other in their efforts to crowd closer into the corner and farther away from the impending rain of fire.

"Speaking of Aschar Coult, which same we were," resumed Denny, having restored discipline, "I've seen forty-seven pictures of Judas Iscariot. No two of 'em looked alike. But every single one of 'em looked enough like Aschar Coult to be his twin brother. He's made you mountain rubes think he's a heller. Well, he ain't. If ever you get back to your own dump, tell the neighbors so. Tell 'em how he said he'd protect you and pay you, for this job, and how he done it. He's played you for suckers, and he's left you holding the bag.

"Now, then," suggested Denny, emphasizing his words by a little shake of the ladle, "here's your one chance: when the troopers comes to gather you in, go with 'em nice. And when you get to the station, come through clean with the story of how Coult sicked you on to kill Mr. Hildreth. Tell the whole thing. The more you tell, the easier the judge is going to make it for you when you come to get tried. Them of you that keeps their mouths shut is due to get life sentences. Them that talks free and tells all they know about Coult and about his sending you down here to finish Mr. Hildreth — why, they are due to get off light. Maybe they'll even be turned loose. They —"

Denny had taken the wrong tack, in his design to make the prisoners confess to the court. He did not understand Jackson White character; nor did he know the mortal terror the average mountaineer feels toward the grip of the Law. To these outdoor folk, the thought of being immured in a cell is unbearable. To them, from childhood, the Law is a thing of matchless dread.

Blayne's forceful reminder of the fate in store for them was unfortunate. It outweighed momentarily their fear of the liquid fire menacing them. By a common impulse the close-packed mass broke its formation and headed

234

toward the doorway.

Denny let out another demoniac war screech, and drew back his arm to hurl the ladle's contents among them. For a moment — if only for a moment — the gesture stayed their flight.

Yet, as it chanced, that moment was enough. For the bolted front door was smashed open. The threshold was filled with blue-clad state troopers; Sergeant Crayne at their head.

"Thank the good Lord you've come!" blithered Denny, all at once limp and panting, as the troopers deftly herded and handcuffed their terror-stricken captives. "Thank the good Lord! You see, for the past five minutes, this lead has been getting cold. It's most as hard as iron, now. There isn't any more danger in it than in a pail of cement. I've been holding up the bunch with a seven-high bobtailed flush. I was ten times as scared as what *they* were. If they had taken a notion to sasshay out of their corner, they could have croaked the both of us and got away clean."

He mopped the chilly sweat from his face; and pattered back into the inner room for the clothing he had discarded while melting the pots of lead for the linotype.

As the last of the prisoners filed out, fettered and cowed, herded by their captors, Blayne came back into the room, drawing a violent pink shirt on, over his head, and beaming about him in complacent triumph.

"Gee!" he remarked, breezily, "I've always

gave the loud ha-ha to folks who said their nerves bothered 'em. But mine sure were playing jitterbug tunes for a few minutes, there. I never knew I had any nerves till then. Lucky those saps weren't printers! Lucky they didn't stop to remember that melted lead don't stay melted forever, in a cool room."

Brant gripped his little partner's hand in wordless appreciation of the shining white pluck that had turned the ghastly crisis. Hildreth's own nerves were raw and jumpy. Reaction was setting in. For the instant, he could not trust his voice to speak. But Denny understood. Wincing under the mighty pressure of the handgrip, he grinned reassuringly up into his partner's blood-streaked face.

"Say!" exclaimed Blayne. "Here I've been blatting about *me,* and I didn't even have the manners to ask how bad you're hurt. I grabbed up the lead pot and the ladle off'n the fire, the second I heard the rumpus out here. But by the time I got here you was down, and most of the population of the lovely blue Ramapo Mountains was drifting up onto you. I saw one of them chaps in the line-up with a jaw that couldn't keep time. Another one of 'em had a bust-in mouth. So you must have handed out a couple of man's-sized wallops before they downed you. But what'd they do to *you?* Are you very bad beat up? Any bones cracked?"

"No," said Hildreth. "I got a knuckle cut on the cheek; and my throat is pretty sore where one of them made an honest try at choking me to death. Then, I feel as if I had a nice assortment of bumps and bruises. But that's all. You see, they didn't come here just to roughhouse me. If they had, I'd have fared worse. As I take it, they only wanted to down me and then cut my throat. So they didn't waste time in slugging or gouging. Coult must have told them to use a knife instead of a gun. A shot would have brought a crowd here. The work had to be done quietly. Some of those mountain men are artists in knifing. If they —"

He and Denny whirled about to face the door. Thane, too, leaped to his feet, growling. The nerves of all three were at frayed tension. The sound of a fumbling hand on the knob was enough to brace the trio for a possible repetition of the onslaught.

Chapter XXVII

Instinctively, Brant laid a restraining hand on Thane's ruff. The door swung slowly open. A disreputable man limped wearily into the room. The bright light made the newcomer screw his eyes to slits. He shut the door behind him and stood just within the threshold.

Unshaven he was, and with dried blood on his dirty face. His clothes were ragged and filthy. His feet were bare. Their soles and insteps were scored as with briars and rock edges. His visage was pallidly sunken from hunger.

"My merry little mountain man," Blayne hailed him, "you're half an hour late to the party. Your playmates have came and they have went. But I'll take you along to 'em. So don't worry, none. They —"

"Melvin!" cried Hildreth, incredulously. "Karl Melvin!"

The visitor's eyes had accustomed themselves to the light. His features were resuming their normal cast. But it required a second keen look to recognize the derelict as the upstanding and neat young athlete of a week earlier.

"Melvin!" echoed Denny, his mouth ajar. "It's —"

Karl slumped into a chair. He seemed about to faint. Blayne ran to the cooler and brought him a glass of water. But already the man had recovered his self-possession. Before touching the glass he spoke hoarsely, in weak excitement.

"Phone for the police!" he croaked. "Quick. They'll be here any minute."

"Who?"

"A bunch of Jackson Whites," croaked Melvin. "That's why I came straight here. I didn't have cash, to phone. They cleaned me out. Money, clothes, everything. I stole this suit, to get away in," he finished, glancing down at the torn and soiled shirt and the ragged trousers, far too small for his bulk.

"It was the Jackson Whites who kidnaped you?" asked Brant. "They —"

"I don't know. I remember I was riding along the Newton road as fast as I could make my bike go. I had had a phone call. I ran into a wire across the road, and I got a bad spill. I was picking myself up, when a crowd of men jumped me. Last thing I knew I was scrapping with them. Then I woke up in a kind of cave. So I knew they must have taken me up into the Ramapos. I hadn't any clothes on and it was dark; and my hammered head hurt me, pretty bad. I don't know how long they kept me up there. I've lost track of time. But they didn't give me anything to eat; and a Jackson White with a rifle sat in front of the cave door all the while. I — Here!" he broke off. "Never mind about *me*. Phone for the police. That crowd will be here any —"

"They've been here," Hildreth reassured him. "And now they're on their way to jail. The troopers have them in tow. Thanks, just the same, from the heart out, for coming to warn us when you're so done up. Rest, till —"

Denny had slipped back into the pressroom. Now he reappeared, carrying a quart bottle, half full of cold black coffee. In his other hand was a thick sandwich.

"Working late tonight," he explained. "So I brought this down to the office, for a snack. Here!"

He proffered the coffee and sandwich to Karl. The starved youth clawed them from him. He drained the pint of strong black coffee without taking the bottle from his cracked lips. Then he wolfed the fat sandwich in two ravenous bites. Almost at once his dulled eyes began to brighten. A ghost of his former ruddy color seeped back into the sunken cheeks. The slumped shoulders squared themselves. Life was returning to the half-dead man.

"Good!" said Melvin. "They got here, and you got them? Good! But I wish I'd been here to take just one crack at them. It was late this afternoon that I crawled to the far back of the cave — it must have been a hundred feet long. I came to where it led out into another cave. All that corner of the Ramapos is thick with caves, you know. Lots of the Jackson Whites have fixed them up to live in. This back opening of the cave had been boarded up, solid. But it must have been a long time ago; because the boards were beginning to rot and there were wormholes through them.

"I could hear a woman in a cave beyond the boards. She was talking to a man who must have been away somewhere and had just got back. For she was telling him things that had happened while he was gone. I suppose he was her husband and that was their cave. I didn't pay much attention. I was too sick and hungry and cold. But by and by I heard her speak about Sheriff Coult. Then I began to listen.

"I couldn't get it all. The boards were too thick. But I got enough to know that Coult had been up there, a day or two ago, and that he told the Jackson Whites that you were aiming to put all their moonshine stills out of business and send the lot of them to prison. He said the only way to keep you from doing it was to kill you. He picked out some of the huskiest of them and he told them to come down here late tonight and knife you. He said if they didn't, you'd pretty soon stamp out the stills and put all the folks up there into the coop. He promised them they'd get good cash and they wouldn't come to any harm, if they'd do the job just the way he told them to.

"That was all I could make out from her talk. I lay there and waited till the cave was quiet.

241

Then I got hold of a sharp stone on the floor; and I pried at the rotten boards. I had to stop every few minutes to see if the man with the rifle, outside my own cave, could hear me. Besides, I was pretty weak. So it was a long job. But I pried one board loose, by and by. That gave me a purchase on the one below it. I peeked out into the other cave. There wasn't anybody in it. I crawled through.

"There was a torn shirt and a pair of greasy pants hanging there. I put them on. I couldn't find any shoes. Then I streaked for here. There were a lot of men and their lanky women sitting round a kind of camp fire, jawing and chattering. Most likely they were waiting up for news of the bunch that had come down here after you. I was scared that I'd be too late. But I wasn't strong enough to go very fast. And I'm not used to bare feet on stony ground, either. A couple of times I lost my way, too. I —"

"You're a white man, Melvin!" declared Brant. "One of God's white men. I shan't forget this. It isn't everyone who would go out of his way to warn us, before he'd even gone home for food and clothes. It —"

"It isn't everyone who'd dive into the pond hole when he didn't know how to swim, just to save my kid sister, the way Blayne did," rejoined Karl. "So that squares that. Now I'm going home. Lend me a dollar, will you? On the way, I'm going to stop at the all-night lunch wagon and eat it empty. Then I'm going to get a bath and a shave and a couple of years' sleep."

"This," said Denny, with much conclusiveness, "this has been one of them nights. I wouldn't 'a' missed it for a thousand dollars. Nor yet I wouldn't go through it again, for a million."

Chapter XXVIII

As early as ten o'clock, on the following Saturday morning, townsfolk and farmers from rural sections of the county began to gather at various points along the Preakness-Hudson Highway, leading into Sark. Folk, too, from as far away as Pompton Lakes and Haverstraw.

The *Bugle* had told of the proposed examination visit to be paid at noon by the state road inspectors from Trenton and by the expert who would announce the result of the core analyses. With its tabulated schedules of the road's specifications and depth of concrete, the paper had been on the street long before nine o'clock.

Within an hour, the news had flown far and wide. Sark people had telephoned it to neighbors, miles away, with an invitation to "drive into town, and see the fun."

The courthouse windows showed no faces. But in Mayor O'Roon's office a knot of worried and fidgeting and frightened-eyed local officials were clustered; discussing the tidings and making and remaking futile suggestions as to how the exposure might be blocked.

Not a man was there who did not know the various lines of lucrative fraud practiced in the building of that stretch of county highway. Not a man there who, directly or indirectly, had not profited thereby.

And, this morning, of all inauspicious times, Aschar Coult was absent. Absent, too, was Ralph Cormick, chairman of the Board of Freeholders. Cormick had gone, at eight o'clock, with Coult, on one of the sheriff's frequent business trips to the Hudson region at the far end of the county. They began the journey before the *Bugle*, with its devastating announcement, was on the streets.

They had driven forth in Coult's car, Mowgli sitting between them as usual. Frantic telephone calls from O'Roon's office to various points along their proposed route had failed to locate them. Thus in a time of stark need, the county leader and his foremost henchman were not to be on hand to bear the brunt of the coming ordeal, nor to devise ways for averting it.

As groups stood gossiping on street corners, there was a general atmosphere of something more than mere idle public curiosity. There was an undercurrent of sternness, of indignation; a general realization of wrong and an intent to down it. More than once, the men in the mayor's office spoke worriedly of this new civic attitude.

"Coult says the public are sheep," O'Roon was grumbling, in reply to Cady's comment on the subtly tremendous change which had come over the county's denizens. "He's wrong. The more you fleece sheep and the more you drive them, the more they'll let you do as you please with them. The public's different. For a long time it will mind its own business and let the administration get away with anything. Then all at once someone will tell it what it knew all along, and it'll listen to him. And presently it'll turn on the very crowd it's been voting for so long. That's happened pretty near everywhere, sooner or later. And now, it's due to happen here, unless Coult can hit on some way of muzzling the *Bugle*. What a cinch the politicians must have had, in the days before there were any newspapers!"

A little before noon the state truck rolled into Sark, with its coring machine sticking forth like a mammoth spur from the tailboard. Business-like men set to work, instantly, on the task which had brought them thither. The first core was cut from the square itself.

"The specifications," said a man near Brant, consulting his copy of the *Bugle*, "call for a depth of exactly eight inches of concrete, here. Let's see how deep the core will be."

As he spoke, the inspector handed over to the analyst a cylinder the machine had just cut from the gray road. The specimen was barely four inches through.

"Fifty per cent stolen, on quantity alone," loudly announced the man alongside Brant. "Even if the quality of cement is up to the mark

— and I have a hunch it won't be."

His hunch proved to be wholly correct. The analyst wrought busily over the cylindrical core; crushing it and subjecting it to one after another of his approved tests. The result proved that the contractors and those behind the job had saved almost as much expense in the grade of their material as in the amount of it.

From spot to spot along the highway, the eager crowd trailing after, moved the inspection truck. With a few minor variations every tapped section of roadway gave the same general analysis as had the first specimen.

Truly, Derek Groot, in his last mortal plan, had struck a jarringly destructive blow to the courthouse gang that he hated! To even the most untaught of the throng of bystanders the tests made clear the crookedness of the road work and of its sponsors.

Late in the afternoon, Brant and Denny left the *Bugle* office on their way to supper. Thane had been lying in the open doorway, drowsily watching the passers-by. To the dog's sensitive perceptions the strange new aura of excitement and indignation in the bulk of those who walked past or who stopped to gossip at the corner was keenly apparent. The thrill of it communicated itself to the collie; as human emotions ever react upon highly sensitized animals.

Wherefore it was with an unwonted eagerness and a fanfare of plangent barks that he sprang up and capered around his masters, as Hildreth and Blayne emerged from the building. The gay barking was heard by another dog. It was accepted by him as a defiance, spurring him into instant action.

Down Sussex Street, on the way home from their drive to the Hudson, came Aschar Coult and Ralph Cormick, Mowgli, the huge police dog, sitting erect and formidable between them. The brass studding on the dog's wide morocco collar sparkled in the soft afternoon sunlight. The dog himself was peering fiercely from left to right, to locate the sound of Thane's clamorous barking.

To Coult there was something unusual, something not at all reassuring, in the aspect of the people the car moved past, in Sussex Street. The looks they gave him and Cormick, their nudges and inaudible comments, disturbed the sheriff. As sensitive as Thane in the reading of others' emotions, Coult sensed an added hostility, a new flame of indignation toward himself.

O'Roon's telephone messages having failed to reach him anywhere along the route, he was ignorant of the surprise visit of the state road inspectors and the result of their tests. Thus he could only surmise that some attack in the day's *Bugle* had stirred up the Sark folk afresh. Gloweringly he surveyed the *Bugle* office and the two men coming out of its doorway.

At the same time, Mowgli's questing gaze focused on the corn-colored collie dancing around Brant's legs. The police dog had not only located the harrowing barks, but had located his enemy as well.

In a diving bound, Mowgli cleared the door of the car and sprang down into the street, before either Cormick or Coult could guess at his intent. He dashed at Thane, teeth bared, head down. The collie saw him, just in time to meet the whirlwind attack.

The two dogs clashed in raging impact, rearing, tearing, snarling at each other. Mowgli attempted a ruse known only to wolves and to police dogs and to collies. As Thane plunged for his forelegs, the larger dog struck downward for the base of the collie's skull, seeking to gain a grip there which should enable his murderous teeth to grind their way through to the spinal cord.

But a collie goes into battle equipped with a well-nigh impervious armor. His ruff, when he is in full coat, is all but toothproof. Mowgli gathered a mouthful of hair and a scrap of skin between his ravening jaws, and practically nothing else.

Twisting like a snake, Thane drove for his enemy's momentarily exposed throat. Deep into the thick morocco collar sank the collie's razor-like incisors and eyeteeth. Mowgli wrenched violently to free himself The wrench only sent Thane's teeth deeper into the collar's soft leather; and tore a rent an inch long in it.

Aschar Coult had sprung from the car and run forward. Now, as in the former clash between Thane and Mowgli, the sheriff caught the police dog by the nape of the neck and jerked him high in air; even as Brant called the collie imperatively from the conflict.

But Brant's summons was not needed. Already, Thane had loosed his collar grip. He was backing away, sneezing and choking. Somehow he seemed to have lost all interest in the fight.

Chapter XXIX

Coult swung the police dog back into the car and deposited him there. Half-subconsciously, Hildreth saw and wondered at a minor phenomenon in regard to this move: When Coult had picked up the dog, the torn morocco collar was still around Mowgli's throat, its brass studs agleam. Yet when he set the dog down, hard, upon the car's seat, the collar was no longer around his neck. During that second or so, it had vanished.

The car was driven away rapidly, Ralph holding the struggling and snarling police dog firmly lest Mowgli attempt another leap from the machine. To avoid the gathering crowd and to see whether or not Thane had incurred any hurt during the brief scrimmage, Hildreth went back into the office, whistling his collie to follow him.

Denny Blayne came in after them, but not until he had squinted wonderingly for an instant at something on the curb.

Blayne found Hildreth examining Thane for possible bite marks. The collie was crouching spiritlessly on the floor, as though he were sick. Occasionally he coughed or sought to clear his throat. Denny watched him for a second, then unceremoniously he brushed past Hildreth and knelt down beside the dog.

He looked carefully at Thane's mouth corners; and he rubbed one side of the collie's face, just back of the jaw. The rub caused a few grains of white powder to be dislodged from the fur around the jaw hinge. Denny caught the grains deftly on the back of his other hand.

He lifted his hand to his face and sniffed experimentally at the powder, drawing it up into his nostrils. For a short space, then, Blayne stood wordless and as in deep cogitation; while Hildreth marked the whitish deposit at the collie's mouth corners and a light scatter of powder which had fallen from his fur to the floor. He glanced from the sick dog up to Blayne. Before he could speak, Denny came to swift and wrathful life.

"Snow!" he yelled. "*Snow!* Wait here!"

He snatched up an envelope from the desk and ran out into the street. At the curb he stopped and knelt down above the object he had stared at a minute earlier. The thing was a little drift of white powder that had fallen there. With meticulous care, Denny scraped into the open envelope as much of it as he could brush up. He went on to the roadway itself, along which Coult had carried Mowgli from the sidewalk to the near-by car.

The entire short route was traced by tiny sprinklings of the white powder. A larger drift

252

of it lay where the dog had been lifted aboard. This second deposit of powder, as well, Blayne brushed into his envelope. His face black with anger, he stamped back into the office and shut the door behind him.

"I never tried the lousy stuff but once," he growled. "I did it then, to see was it so wonderful as they said it was. And it wasn't. I've laid off'n it, ever since. But that once was enough to let me know it, if ever I tackled it again. And I've lived all my life where some folks will sell their wedding rings and their gold teeth, to say nothing of their puny souls, for a sniff of it. Lord, but I hate it worse'n I hate Aschar Coult! I've seen too much of what it can do."

"What on earth are you blithering about?" demanded Hildreth, annoyed by the mystery of the little East-sider's words and actions.

"Snow!" snorted Blayne. "I'm talking about SNOW. 'Cocaine's' the fancy name for it. That stuff on Thane's mouth. This stuff I put into the envelope here. This specimen goes to the first square chemist I can find; to prove what I know already. Not that I'm needing proof. But the law may."

Aghast, Brant Hildreth listened. Bit by bit he began to understand.

"Snow!" reiterated Denny. "Or cocaine, if you like the big word. The folks that's wrecked by it calls it 'snow.' Just as they say 'junk' when they mean 'heroin.' Snow and junk has done more harm than ever any war did. I'm no crank, Lord knows. But when it comes to drugs, I've saw too much of the hell they can make, to be able to talk nice and ca'm about 'em. Travel with the bunch I used to train with, and live in the places I used to live in — and you'll feel just the way I do about the stuff."

"But —" stammered Brant, "but how — ?"

"You was too busy getting Thane out of that fight to do much noticing," explained Denny. "But I saw something. And I saw it so plain I can take oath on it. Thane gets a holt onto that big padded soft-leather collar the other dog's wearing. The collar rips open for maybe an inch. Just then Coult lifts the dog up. Out from that rip in the collar sifts a lot of white powder. I saw it and I can swear to it."

"*What?*"

"More'n once I've noticed that fine wide thick collar on Cormick's police dog," Denny raged on. "And more'n once I've wondered why folks would want to make a poor critter so uncomf't'ble by having him tote such a mon-strous wadded thing around his neck. Now, I know. That collar is fixed up, inside, like it was a money belt. Likely it's stuffed with cotton or something, when it ain't in use. Then when Cormick and Coult goes to wherever they go to get the snow that's smuggled in from Europe, the cotton is took out, and the collar is crammed full of dope. They was just back from such a trip this afternoon, the two of 'em."

"They — they're —"

"They're a pair of dope smugglers!" rasped Denny, his voice hoarse with contemptuous ire. "That's what they are — Coult and our high-hat 'ristocrat friend, Ralphy. Dope smuggling is about the dangerousest breed of law-busting there is. Partly because no halfway decent feller will help out in it. There's plenty of sympathy for bootleggers and rumrunners and diamond smugglers. But no decent man or woman has any sympathy for dope-handling. It's like kidnaping, that way. All the world is against a kidnaper. And all the world is against the dope traffic.

"It's the dangerousest crook-trade there is; but it's the best paying. A single suitcase full of junk or snow or morphia will sell for twice as much as a steamship full of booze. That dog collar must hold easy a pound of dope. There's more profit in it than in whole truckloads of bootleg stuff.

"But there's more danger, too. So our two noble friends makes sure they won't be caught with the goods, if they're held up and searched. They put it in a dog collar. Nobody's going to search a dog for dope. It's as safe as a church. Or it was, till Thane tore a hole in the collar. No wonder the poor collie looks sick! He must have sucked a swad of it into his nose and mouth. He'll be all right, presently. Now, I'm going to chase over to Wegel's drugstore and make Sol Wegel analyze this while I wait. He's square; and he's a good chemist. Likewise and also he hates Coult.

"I'll tell him the whole thing. He'll do the analyzing, and he'll give us an affidavit. There ain't a judge, anywheres — not even Pinky Bogardus — that'll dare refuse to make out a warrant for the arrest of two drug smugglers, when we've got the goods on 'em, like we've got on Cormick and Aschar Coult.

"Plenty of folks saw me brushing up that powder in the street. They can prove I didn't plant it there. The *Bugle* needn't have wasted so much thunder on those two. This stunt alone is enough to bust the courthouse gang to flinders and to send its two bosses over the road for a mighty long stretch. I'll be back as soon as I get this analyzed."

He was gone. Brant Hildreth sank down into his desk chair and buried his face in his folded arms. Victory had come to him, at last — victory and the destruction of the gang of grafters who had bled Preakness County. The enemy was crushed. The way was cleared for wise and clean government. It was a moment for rapturous joy.

And Hildreth's heart was heavy as lead.

To punish Coult and Cormick, he must also strike to the very soul of Kay. Her brother — her only near relative — would be branded as a criminal of the most filthily revolting type. Ralph would be sentenced to prison. Kay's cherished family name would be rolled in the muck, her pride along with it. She would be publicly shamed — heartbroken.

And how would she regard the man to whom her loved brother's disgrace and punishment were due — the man who adored her and yet who had torn her life and her sweet contentment to shreds? She would abhor the very thought of Hildreth. Never again would she consent to speak to him; to look at him. He had won his campaign at the expense of his own future happiness; at cost of all he held precious.

How long he sat there, stonily wretched, he did not know. Once or twice, Thane whimpered softly and strove to thrust his muzzle against his master's buried face. The sunset deepened into early summer dusk. Still Brant crouched over his desk, stricken and numb.

Then Denny Blayne was back again, gleefully waving the analysis report of the chemist, and the affidavit.

"I'm hopping the eight-forty train," he declared. "I'm going to Trenton. I'm going to get hold of Judge Van Sluyk and spill this to him. He'll have the warrants sworn out, first thing in the morning, by whoever does that kind of thing at the capital, and he'll have the right officers come up here to make the arrests. No sense risking a getaway by getting some local judge to make out the warrants. Always go to the top man. That's my rule. So long, Brant! I'll just about have time to make that train, if I sprint. See you tomorrow."

He was gone; fiercely jubilant with the zest of victory.

Too late now to turn back. Too late now to seek to hush the scandal or to avert the punitive blow. The matter was out of Brant's hands. Henceforth he was to be only a spectator at the fulfillment of his own tediously long efforts. He was the winner, and he was unhappier than ever before in all his busy life.

Presently, Hildreth arose, his face marble-set, his lips a thin line. Unheeded by him, the fast-recuperating Thane trotted out of the office at his master's heels. Through the town strode Brant, looking neither to right nor to left, blind and deaf to the occasional greetings bestowed on him by passers-by. He was headed toward a house he had not entered in nearly eight years.

Kay sat, in the fragrant summer darkness, on the vine-shrouded veranda of the old Cormick home. In the lighted study behind her, Ralph was at work over some county papers. He had been a worse than cheerless dinner companion that evening. The tidings of the road graft's exposure had filled him with an uncontrolled fury, through which ran a thread of genuine terror.

True, Aschar Coult had pooh-poohed the whole thing when, stopping at the courthouse on their way home after the dogfight, they had learned the black details of the state inspectors' work. Coult had made light of the peril, but

Ralph had seemed to read under the sheriff's loud reassurance a hint of stark worry.

Cormick himself had less than no practical knowledge of such matters as road building — and indeed of most of the technicalities connected with his office as chairman of the county's Board of Freeholders. Coult was the practical man of the organization. Coult made the contracts and looked out for the details. His subordinates were mere puppets to the overlord who appointed them or had them elected to their various plump offices. Ralph was no exception. Nor did he desire to be.

Cormick knew vaguely that there was much graft in the county. But long ago he had been given to understand that there was as much graft everywhere, and that it was an inseparable adjunct to practical politics. He did not approve of it. Nor, personally, did he consent to profit thereby. His own means rendered him independently well-to-do. But his successive county offices, awarded to him through Coult's friendship, had been gratifying to his vanity. And they had enhanced his prestige as a lawyer.

He had resented angrily Brant Hildreth's campaign to upset local customs. He regarded the editor as a decidedly objectionable and visionary reform crank. This feeling was abetted tenfold by his early causeless dislike for Hildreth.

Chapter XXX

As Kay sat looking out into the soft darkness, a man and a collie dog turned in at the gate and came rapidly up the walk. There was an unbidden thrill at Kay's heartstrings, as she recognized Hildreth's stocky figure and wide shoulders. For no logical reason, her breath came fast and irregularly.

Then, as she arose and ran forward to meet the visitor, she reflected that Brant could scarcely have chosen a less auspicious time to call. Ralph had been railing viciously about him, all through dinner. And now Ralph was sitting in the study behind her. Through the open window the lamplight was streaming. There was certain to be an uncomfortable scene, should her brother discover Hildreth was there.

Thane gamboled forward to the advancing girl, frisking around her and claiming a word of friendliness. She stooped to pet him and speak to him. Then with both hands outstretched she hailed Brant.

"I'm so glad!" she said, simply. "Ever so glad, Brant! Always I've been hoping you'd come to see me . . . Let's go out into the garden, shan't we? It's cooler there than on the porch or indoors. The —"

She caught sight of his ice-grim face, in the shift of lamplight from the study window.

"What is it?" she asked, frightened. "What is wrong? Tell me."

"I didn't come to see you," answered Hildreth, resisting with terrific effort a crazy yearning to catch her up into his arms and to tell her all she was to him. "I came to see your brother. Whether he wants to see me or not. Will you please tell him it is on *his* business that I want to see him, not on mine? Whether he'll consent to see me or not, I must —"

A shadow fell athwart the window's radiance. Cormick stepped out on the veranda. He had heard the murmur of voices and he had recognized Hildreth's tones. Blackly irate, he strode forth and walked up to the visitor, fists clenched, eyes ablaze.

"I told you," he said thickly, "I told you to keep away from my home. Now you'll take the consequences of disobeying that warning. I —"

"Ralph!" pleaded Kay, vehemently.

But Hildreth intervened, before she could say more.

"Won't you please leave me alone with your brother?" he begged her. "My business with him is —"

"You can have no business with me, at all!" snapped Cormick. "Kay, you'll stay where you are. It won't take me more than half a minute to get rid —"

"Of prison?" supplemented Brant. "I'm afraid it will take you many years. Unless you care to listen to me. That is why I'm here. I'm sorry to speak this way where your sister is. But you insist on her staying, and my errand with you can't wait. I am here to try to save you from arrest, Cormick. Now do you want to hear what I have to say, or do you still want me to go?"

"You'll go!" thundered Cormick, taking a step forward and brushing aside the girl who tried piteously to intervene between the two angered men. "And if you think a Preakness County jury will convict a Cormick because some sub-contractor failed to live up to all his road specifications —"

"I don't," returned Brant, forcing himself to a semblance of coolness. "But I know that a *Federal* jury anywhere in the United States will convict you or anyone else who is proven to be a drug smuggler. And by this time tomorrow morning a Federal warrant will be out, for your arrest on that charge. I came to warn you — to give you a chance to get across the Canadian border and to go into hiding; until your friends can try to soften the sentence that's certain to be passed on you. Now —"

He paused. Even in that uncertain light, Brant could see the expression of unfeigned astonishment on Cormick's face. The look told more than a volume of protestations.

Brant Hildreth drew a long breath of relief.

This man was not guilty of the foul charge against him. To that, Hildreth could have sworn. No actor could have simulated such blankly ignorant bewilderment at so short a notice.

"Drug smuggling?" sputtered Cormick. "What idiocy are you blithering? Are you drunk?"

"Do you care to hear what I have to say?" repeated Brant. "Or do you still want me to go?"

Sharply, in the dimness of the lawn, Ralph Cormick eyed his unwelcome visitor. Kay still hovered between the men and peered anxiously from one to the other. Then —

"Come in!" said Ralph, curtly. "I don't understand any of this. It may be a trick. But nobody's going to leave my house with that damnable opinion of me. Come in, and tell me what you're driving at."

In the bright-lit study, with Kay listening in ever-growing horror, Brant told his story. He told it briefly, yet omitting no detail.

As Hildreth proceeded, Ralph Cormick's dark face grew ever blacker and more enraged. He was enough of a man of the world and enough of a lawyer to see that Hildreth was not making up the amazing tale nor digging into a mare's nest.

Trembling with fury Cormick heard him through. Then, as Brant finished by telling of the analyzing of the cocaine and of Denny's night trip to the state capital, Cormick found his tongue.

"I see the whole thing!" he blazed. "And this isn't the first nor the fifth time it has happened. Coult asked me to go with him on his trip to the river. While I was at lunch, a boy from a sloop at the dock came in — as he had come, other times — to say the sloop's captain would like a word with Coult, on board. Coult told me to go on with my lunch and that he'd be right back. He whistled to Mowgli to go along with him. They were back again in less than ten minutes. I — well, I didn't actually know it, but I have always had an idea that Coult makes a little extra money by indirect dealings with the rumrunners. So I supposed it was something like that the captain wanted to talk over with him. Neither of us spoke of it afterward, of course, and —"

"And he took *you* along!" cried Kay, in hot indignation. "He took *you* along on these drug-smuggling trips, to whitewash him and to throw off any chance of suspicion! Everyone would know that Ralph Cormick couldn't have a hand in such a vile thing. So your being with him would shield him, in case —"

"The swine!" raged Cormick, this new aspect of the case sinking into his consciousness and redoubling his wrath, as he realized the dupe role he had been made to play. "The swine! The cocaine was hidden in the collar of my own dog, too. In case of discovery, that would shift the blame from Coult to me. Coult would swear the dog was mine, and that he didn't know anything about Mowgli's trick collar. There's a bill to pay for this!"

He strode to the telephone, snatching up the receiver.

"What are you going to do?" asked Kay, worried.

"I'm going to find out if Aschar Coult is at home!" fumed Ralph. "If he is, I'm going to his house. And Hildreth is going with me. This thing is going to be settled inside of ten minutes, if — Hello! Ralph Cormick speaking. Is Mr. Coult at home?" he called.

He listened for a moment, then slammed the receiver back in place and turned to Brant and Kay.

"His housekeeper says Coult drove to New York, an hour ago, on business," Cormick reported. "He left word he'd be back in time for eight o'clock breakfast, in the morning. He told her to have it ready at eight, sharp, because he has a busy day ahead of him."

"He has," assented Brant. "I suppose she didn't say where a message would reach him in New York?"

"She didn't know. The best we can do is to be at his house when he gets back in the morning. Will you go there with me?"

"Yes," promised Hildreth, "though it would be wiser to wait till the police can get there from Trenton, as soon as the warrant is issued. They ought to reach Sark by ten o'clock or so. If he's put on his guard —"

"The police can have what's left, when I'm through with him," said Cormick. "He and I have got to settle our own private account before then. I'll stop by at your house for you at seven-thirty. That will get us to Coult's in time to nail him as he gets out of his car for breakfast."

"You won't do anything rash — anything foolish, Ralph?" implored Kay. "Brant, you won't let him — ?"

"My people helped to settle this region," answered Ralph. "Cormicks have been the leaders here for more than two hundred years. And Aschar Coult has done his best to put a foul smear on the memory of them all, and to send me to prison on the dirtiest charge that could be made against me. To use me as a cat's-paw and to go free while I take the blame that's his! That isn't on the free list, Kay. He's got to settle with me for it. Besides, the same officers who arrest him will arrest me. Then it'll be too late for me to —"

"*No!*" cried his sister. "No! Oh, Brant, he *won't* be arrested, too, will he? Please —"

"If you'll let me use that phone," answered Brant, "I'll call up Judge Van Sluyk, on long distance. Denny won't have gotten to him, yet. Van Sluyk is a power in Trenton. I am going to explain this whole thing to him, and I am going to do it in a way to make him see you were the ignorant dupe and that you had nothing at all to do with the drug smuggling or — By the way, did Coult give you that collar for Mowgli, or did you — ?"

"Mr. Coult used it for him when he still owned Mowgli," said Kay. "He kept it as a mascot, he said. He said he had an idea it brought him luck. So he used to carry it around in one of his big coat pockets, and he'd only put it on Mowgli when he and the dog were going somewhere together. Several people can testify to that. He —"

"Good!" approved Hildreth. "That ought to be proof enough to convince Van Sluyk that Coult engineered the whole thing. But your brother will have to appear as a witness, I suppose. Now if I may use the phone —"

Fifteen minutes later, Hildreth turned from the instrument, to report to the brother and sister the result of his talk with Van Sluyk, and to give the judge's assurance that Cormick would be held, for the present, only as a material witness, and would be admitted to low bail on his pledge to tell in court all he knew.

But much may occur within the short space of fifteen minutes.

During that time a demure-faced butler had stepped noiselessly from the dining room which was separated only by drawn curtains from the library. Slipping from the house he had run all the way to Aschar Coult's home. There, he had babbled excitedly a tale and a warning to Coult's housekeeper.

Chapter XXXI

Next morning, a little after half-past seven, Ralph Cormick and Hildreth drove in the former's runabout up the road leading to Aschar Coult's. As they were within fifty yards of the front gate, another runabout came whizzing out through the gateway. Aschar Coult was at the wheel. The machine whirled sharply into the highroad, heading away from Cormick and Brant, and roared off at a sixty-mile pace.

Instantly, Cormick ground his foot down upon his own car's accelerator and dashed in pursuit.

"He's been warned!" cried Ralph. "He got home a few minutes ago, and someone there told him what was up. I know it. For he saw me and recognized me, when I waved to him, just now. But he never stopped. And I saw faces looking out of the downstairs windows, after him. He's escaping. He is making for the New York line and the Canada road."

Cormick said no more, but put on all speed the car could compass. Through the sunnily quiet summer morning flew the two machines, Coult a bare furlong in the lead.

Along level stretches, around sharp corners,

up steep hills and down again sped the racers. Bit by bit the sheriff's car began to draw away from its pursuer. Now a quarter-mile or more gaped between the two.

"I wonder how much gas I've got!" grunted Ralph, once. "I wish I'd thought to ask. This gas gauge is out of order. But I'll get him and I'll bring him back, if I have to make it on foot."

It was the only time either he or Hildreth spoke, during that many-mile run. A final long curve, and Greenwood Lake came into view, flashing fire-blue in the sunlight. Two miles farther, along its edge, was the New York State line. A bare mile across the lake itself was New York State. Into the final two-mile stretch turned the cars, Coult's machine perhaps five hundred yards in advance.

Then through the still air and above the hum of Ralph's car, sounded an explosion. At first, Brant thought the sheriff had opened fire on them. But he saw Coult's car twist perilously toward the ditch; right itself by a wrench of its driver's hand at the wheel, and begin to bump heavily.

Hildreth knew then that the pistol-like report had been the sound of a blowout. Ralph laughed aloud in fierce exaltation, as he bore down upon the crippled runabout.

Coult brought his car to a lurching halt alongside a rustic dock, near a roadhouse. He sprang to earth and dashed for the dock. Two canoes lay there, with paddles alongside them. The sheriff drove his heel through the canvas bottom of one. He picked up the other and launched it, seizing a paddle and lowering himself into the cranky red craft.

At the same moment, Ralph brought his car to a standstill, alongside the dock. Well did both that car's occupants understand Coult's ruse. The New York shore was hardly a mile away. The road, for a long distance on the far side of the lake, was torn up for repairs. It was impassable to cars. By crossing the lake in one of the canoes — first putting the other out of commission to avert pursuit — Coult could win the safety of the northernmost Ramapo Hills. Thence, born mountaineer as he was, he could readily elude capture in that all-but-impenetrable region; and he could either bide his time to get to Canada from the nearest train line or else he could work his way eastward to the Jackson Whites who joyfully would hide and protect their demigod.

Brant Hildreth was out of the car, before Ralph could bring it to a full halt. To the dock he ran, pulling his coat off as he went. Bunching the garment into a tight mass he shoved the improvised caulking into the hole which Coult's heel had torn in the second canoe's bottom. It was a wretchedly bad water gap; but it might perhaps serve for a minute or two. He lifted the canoe down into the water, boarded it, and sent it spinning out into the lake with a flail-like succession of short paddle strokes.

After the first canoe darted the second; while Ralph Cormick strained cursingly to launch a leaky scow he had found under the dock.

Aschar Coult was a giant in stature and in physical strength, but his knowledge of paddling a canoe was little more than rudimentary. That is a gift which calls for deft practice, far more than for brute strength. And this deft practice Hildreth possessed to a somewhat unusual degree. On his mantelshelf in his mother's home stood two small silver cups won by him at college in canoe races. There they flanked his "amateur heavyweight-boxer" cup.

Despite the drag of the coat-bulge beneath the keel and despite the ever-increasing seepage of water through the porous garment into the bottom of the canoe, he was gaining on his quarry at every skilled stroke. Moreover, he was a full forty pounds lighter than Coult. And weight counts in such a contest. Straining every nerve, Brant made his craft leap through the quiet waters like a live thing; easily cutting down the distance that lay between.

Aschar Coult, splashing and heaving at his paddle, heard the smooth onrush of his foe. He glanced over his shoulder. The other canoe was almost alongside. Coult gave a sidewise tug to his paddle, which sent his canoe spinning broadside to the oncomer.

At the same time he aimed a mighty downward sweep of the paddle at Hildreth's head, as the two fragile craft crashed together.

Hildreth ducked the blow and flung himself forward, gripping Coult around the middle. The sheriff beat murderously at his antagonist's head with both fists. Promptly, the canoe turned turtle. The furiously grappling fighters reeled overboard with a resounding splash. They sank below the surface, close locked in deadly embrace.

Down, down they sank, stiff twisting and smiting and wrestling. Brant, by swimmer's instinct, had gulped a mouthful of air as his canoe upset. He had dire need of it. For Coult's huge fingers had found Hildreth's throat. Their vise-pressure was strangling him; biting deep into the firm flesh of his neck as they felt for the jugular.

Ordinarily Brant would have countered this hold by driving a series of short-arm blows with both fists against Coult's unguarded heart and wind; or by trying to land an effective hook to the equally unguarded jaw. But, under water, arms and hands move with nightmare slowness and inefficiency, save only for propelling one's own body.

The life was being crushed out of Hildreth by that awful throat grip. Now the diggingly exploring fingers of one of Coult's hands had found the carotid. In another moment, Brant must be rendered helpless, if not killed outright, by the gigantic strength and prowess of those hands.

More by instinct than by reason, Brant doubled himself into a ball, his feet against Coult's expansive midsection. Then, with his last remaining rally of strength, he threw his whole weight and trained muscles into a convulsively sudden straightening out of his whole body.

Coult had him by the throat. Brant's feet thus formed the other end of a human catapult as he yanked himself rigidly straight. The leverage enabled the sheriff's gripping fingers well-nigh to tear Hildreth's throat out.

But, in the same instant, those fingers loosed their hold. The tremendous snapping double impact of Brant's heels into the solar plexus had had the wonted effect of a well-delivered solar plexus blow. It had sent a paralysis throughout its victim's entire giant body; a paralysis which, ordinarily may last anywhere from seconds to minutes before its first shock passes off.

Feebly Brant's hands and tinglingly aching legs beat the water downward. Up, with agonizing slowness, crept his tortured body toward the surface, through the shimmeringly green underwater.

His throat was in torment. He was spent and broken. Vaguely he felt his head emerge from beneath the surface. He tried to draw a long breath. The effort was intolerable.

In a blur he saw someone propelling a clumsy

scow toward him, using a broken plank for an oar.

Then Brant became wholly engrossed in an effort to keep his nostrils above the waterline. The task was more than he could compass. His strength was gone and his torn throat was on fire. Slowly he sank.

For centuries Brant Hildreth continued to sink helplessly through millions of miles of soft blackness. Then pain renewed its dominion over him.

After an interminable time he slept.

Slowly, very very slowly, he awoke. He was not at the bottom of Greenwood Lake. He was not even in his own room. He was in a room he never before had seen — a dainty room of pale blues and pinks and with white window curtains which billowed in the breeze.

Over him was bending someone — a woman. It was Kay Cormick.

He blinked dazedly at her, noting with dull amaze the flood of utter happiness and relief which swept across her face as she saw him return to his senses.

"Hush!" she whispered, her dear hand light and cool on his racked forehead. "You mustn't talk. Ralph lifted you out of the lake, just as you were sinking. Dr. Vreeland worked over you, and he said you were out of danger. Then Ralph brought you home to us. You're in my room. Lie perfectly still. Dr. Vreeland will be here again in a minute."

"Coult?" whispered Brant, incoherently.

"Mr. Coult — didn't come to the surface again," she answered, with a reminiscent little shudder; adding, "Now don't try to talk. Go to sleep."

Obediently he closed his tired eyes. His breathing grew slow and regular. Then, he felt once more that she was bending over him.

Softly, something brushed his lips. The touch went through him like the breath of God. It brought him to himself with an incredulous cry of delight.

"Kay!" he babbled.

She shrank back, scarlet; faltering:

"I — I thought you were asleep."